Grows That Way

# Grows That Way

by

## Susan Ketchen

OOLICHAN BOOKS
FERNIE, BRITISH COLUMBIA, CANADA
2012

Library and Archives Canada Cataloguing in Publication

Ketchen, Susan

    Grows that way / Susan Ketchen.

ISBN 978-0-88982-285-6

    I. Title.

PS8621.E893G76 2012    jC813'.6    C2012-900604-1

We gratefully acknowledge the financial support of the Canada Council for the Arts, the British Columbia Arts Council through the BC Ministry of Tourism, Culture, and the Arts, and the Government of Canada through the Canada Book Fund, for our publishing activities.

Published by
Oolichan Books
P.O. Box 2278
Fernie, British Columbia
Canada V0B 1M0

www.oolichan.com

Cover photograph by Isobel Springett, www.isobelspringett.com.

MIX
Paper from
responsible sources
FSC
www.fsc.org
FSC® C013916

For Mike

# chapter
## one

Logan Losino is walking beside me. He's wearing his goofy knit cap pulled down over his ears, even though the sun is shining and we won't have snow for at least another month.

We're on our way to school. So why aren't I riding my bike?

My horse Brooklyn is walking behind us. I can feel his warm breath on the back of my neck as though he's looking for an opportunity to sneak between me and Logan, but we're walking so close together this isn't going to happen.

I'm wondering where I can put Brooklyn while I'm in class all day and whether I could tie him to my locker, and that's when I realize I must be dreaming—lucid dreaming, my specialty.

In lucid dreams I am in control and can do anything I want, which makes them different from my regular dreams, and from my regular life come to think of it. In lucid dreams I could probably even fly but usually I dream about riding horses. When I was younger, meaning a couple of months ago, these dreams were less realistic, sometimes even including a unicorn, but I've outgrown that sort of thing now. Still, I have no idea why I'm dreaming about Logan Losino.

I feel his fingers fumbling for mine, and then we're holding hands.

Did I want that?

I look up at Logan. He's grown. I decide to make myself the same height as him, something that will never happen in the real world because I have Turner Syndrome and I will always be a shrimp. I suppose I could make Logan shorter instead of making me taller, but that doesn't seem fair. And it's fun to be the height of a normal human being for a change. It's almost like walking on stilts.

Logan smiles at me through his mustache. Mustache? When did Logan grow a mustache? All I remember him having is a faint line of fuzz. I don't even like mustaches. My dad grew one last summer and I made him shave it off because he looked like Hitler and then his upper lip looked diseased because it wasn't tanned like the rest of his face.

"I like your beard," says Logan.

I have a beard? My free hand flies to my face. I do have a beard. It's soft and furry under my fingers. Great. More hair. I already have extra due to my low hairline at the back of my head, but at least that's hidden, and besides I like to think of it as my mane so I don't mind it too much. Face hair would be way different. I feel kind of panicky, but then I notice that Logan really does like my beard, and he's acting as though it's normal for a girl to have a beard. I guess it's okay. And it's only a dream. At least I'm pretty sure it's a dream.

Logan Losino is leaning towards me and his lips are puckered as though he's going to kiss me and just in time Brooklyn sticks his great long head in between us so I guess Logan kisses him instead, and I feel an uncomfortable mish-mash of relief and disappointment at the same time. I hate feeling confused. It's how I feel a lot of the time when I'm awake. I start thinking that maybe I'm not in a dream at all, and that Brooklyn will be running loose on the school grounds while I'm inside being ridiculed for my beard.

I feel so upset that I wake up. It was only a dream. I stroke my cheek to be sure. Skin. Soft plain skin. Thank goodness.

Dad is rushing out the door when I arrive at the breakfast table. He's late as usual but throws me a kiss.

Mom is standing at the counter quietly sipping a coffee. She's still in her dressing gown.

"You okay, Mom? Not going to work today?"

"I'm taking a mental health day," says Mom. "It's important for psychotherapy professionals to model good self-care."

"And it's different from skipping out?" I'm not trying to be a smart aleck. Really, I'd like to know the difference between skipping out and taking some mental health time. But Mom doesn't hear it that way.

She frowns at me. "Of course I'm not skipping out. That would be irresponsible."

"Okay, Mom." I pour some Shreddies into my bowl and add milk until they start to float.

I hear the garage door opening, and the faint purr as Dad starts his car, followed by a lot of crashing grinding noise. Mom spills coffee on the counter as she puts down her mug. And I remember I was in a hurry last night and didn't put my bike away in its designated parking spot beside our paper recycling bin. I was going to move it after dinner and I forgot.

"Oh no," I say. I want to slide under the breakfast table. I want this to be a dream, something that I can change, or something that won't be real when I wake up. I need my bike desperately, not so much for riding to school as for riding to the boarding stable where I keep Brooklyn.

Dad flings open the back door and fastens his eyes on me immediately even though I've leaned in behind the cereal box.

"You left your bike behind the Explorer!" he yells.

"You didn't look?" Mom asks him. "You didn't check your mirrors?"

The fire-breathing dragon turns in her direction. "I will not be criticized by someone who drives a car that can park itself." My mom has a new Prius. Dad's right, it has a computer that can take over when you're parking, though Mom is afraid to use it—she says she doesn't like giving up control to a car.

"But Dad," I say, "Mom never uses the computer, she always parks manually."

"So wasn't that a total waste of money!" Dad yells at Mom.

Maybe I can slink off to my room without anyone noticing. I ease my butt off the chair.

"There's no need to raise your voice, Tony. That never solves anything," says Mom. She picks up her mug and takes a sip of coffee as though nothing major is wrong. She could be right about that. No one's died. At least not yet. Though Dad looks like he's brewing an aneurism. Probably I should follow Mom's example and stay calm. This is what Kansas always tells me too, when I'm out at the barn. I settle my seat bones back on the chair, square my shoulders and lift my head as though there's a line pulling it up to the sky, just like how I ride: balanced and ready for anything.

"Don't you expect me to drive her to school now," says Dad, stabbing a finger in Mom's direction. "I'm late as it is, and it's about time she started to suffer the consequences of her behaviour."

This is odd. He's sounding more like Mom. The

psychobabble must be contagious. What would be more normal would be for Dad to be complaining about the cost of fixing what used to be a perfectly good bike.

"I can drive her," says Mom. "I'm not going in to work today. I'm taking a mental health day."

"She's modeling good self-care," I tell Dad, hoping he'll pick up the hint and do some deep breathing before his own head explodes.

Dad looks back and forth between me and Mom as though he can't decide which of us is the greater enemy. I feel sick when he settles on me, and only barely manage to hold my balanced posture. I stretch my neck taller, and Dad glares at me. He's never done this before. Usually when he loses his temper it's because the computer has seized up, or because he and Mom are arguing. I've never been the focus, so haven't noticed before how small his eyes become as they sink back into his head, and how his lips get so thin that his mouth disappears, and the only thing left of his face is a great big nose. It's as if he's transformed into a totally different person or some sort of predatory bird with a beak specially designed for tearing apart small animals. I don't know whether to laugh or cry.

He grabs the Shreddies box and flings it at the counter, leaving me totally open to attack. "You will walk to school, Sylvia."

Instead of pecking me to death, he pivots and slams the door behind him. Through the kitchen window I see my bike airborne before it lands in a tangled heap on the lawn.

I pick up my spoon and swirl it through my untouched breakfast. There are ripples in the milk that make me realize my fingers are trembling. I've totally lost my appetite, but Mom will insist I eat everything because breakfast is the most important meal of the day. I can't believe this has happened. It's the first time that using my balanced confident riding posture hasn't helped me with a difficult situation. This time, if it did anything, it made matters worse.

I take a peek at Mom who is watching from behind the curtain as Dad backs out the driveway. I'm not sure, but I think there are tears in her eyes. I so wish I'd put my bike away like I was supposed to.

"Mom, I'm sorry."

She wipes the spilled coffee from the countertop. When she turns to face me, there's no sign of tears so I guess it was just how the light came in the window.

"It's good that you apologize, Sweetie. You made a mistake by not putting your bike away properly. But I hope you're not apologizing for anything else, because that display was not an example of effective parenting."

I feel like I've entered an alternate universe. I can't remember Mom openly criticizing Dad's parenting before. They have a rule about being a team and working together and presenting a united front at all times. Maybe in this universe I don't have to go to school. It's worth a try.

"Mom, do I really have to walk to school? I don't know if I have time. I could stay home with you today. If I'm late Mr. Brumby won't let me into class anyway."

Mom knows about Mr. Brumby and how he rules his class with an iron hand. She doesn't approve of his methods, she says he has no grasp of motivation theory. So she nods sympathetically but then says, "It won't hurt you to walk, Cookie. I think it would be wise to go along with your dad on this, tactically speaking. He's not exactly wrong about you experiencing the consequences of your behaviour."

I see the united front is re-forming, which is a comfort in a way. At least it's familiar. But the rest of what she said is very strange. Tactics? Usually Mom preaches openness and honesty. I couldn't count the number of times she's told me and Dad that all family secrets are toxic and pathological.

"Shouldn't there be consequences for Dad's behaviour too? Why did he have to get so mad at me?"

"I'm not sure," says Mom. "It probably had nothing to do with you. I expect it's some sort of displacement behaviour. And when people give in to their shadow sides..." She sighs heavily and stares out the window towards the pile of metal that used to be my bike. She becomes so lost in thought that she doesn't complete her lecture, not that it would have helped. Even when she explains herself I usually don't have a clue what she's talking about.

Though I am relieved I wasn't the real cause of Dad's anger, I wonder what else could be going on. I try to remember the last time I caught my parents hugging. Mom won't discuss this with me, she'll say it's private, which is somehow different from a secret, though don't ask me how. I can only hope that as part of her mental health day she will drop by Auntie Sally's for a talk and a glass of wine.

"What about after school?" I say. "I want to go to the barn and ride Brooklyn today. Kansas is going to give me a jumping lesson."

Mom shakes her head. "Sorry, Honey, I'll give Kansas a call a let her know you have to postpone. We'll discuss it more tonight. Hopefully your father will be in a better mood." She checks her watch. "You better get a move on if you don't want to be late." She tops up her coffee, saunters to the table, pulls out a chair and sits down. I take my bowl of cereal to the sink and flush it down the garburator and Mom doesn't say a word. This is so not like her. It's like she's on drugs. I think they're both on drugs. Mom's on some sort of tranquilizer, and I have no idea what my dad's on, but something. Too bad there wasn't something that worked for me.

# chapter
## two

I used to be on drugs. For a while I took human growth
hormone, because I am so short from the Turner Syndrome.
But it increased my intracranial pressure, which gave me
headaches and double vision, which made me crash my bike
when I was doubling my cousin Taylor, who got her big toe
caught in the chain and cut it off, leaving her a cripple
unable to pursue her true-life passion of dancing. Now she's
decided to become an animal communicator instead. She's
practicing on her dog Bunga, who is so stupid I can't see why
anyone would want to communicate with him psychically
or otherwise. She's also practicing on Spike, who is very very
scary smart. He's a hinny, which is kind of like a mule, only
he's a hybrid of a male horse and a female donkey. Mules are
hybrids of a male donkey and a female horse. Spike used to
belong to me, but Taylor wanted him when I got Brooklyn.
Brooklyn The Magnificent. Who I don't get to see today
because my dad ran over my stupid bike.

When I've been off the growth hormone for another
month or so I'm going to start on estrogen therapy, so I can
develop secondary sexual characteristics. My mom has already
bought me a brassiere, a fake padded one she thinks I should

wear in the interim, but I say no thanks. To me, bras look too much like harnesses, or like the halter I put on Brooklyn's head, but with more lacey bits. Mom acts like I should be all excited about acquiring secondary sexual characteristics, which doesn't make sense to me, even though it would make me normal. From what I see at school, normal doesn't impress me very much. Fake padded normal would be even worse.

To be honest, I did wear the bra once, but only to get Mom off my back. There's no way I was going to wear it to school, because I'm sure somehow Amber would notice and make a big deal of it and embarrass me to death. Instead I wore it on a Saturday, to a riding lesson, which was a big mistake. Maybe I didn't have the straps tight enough, but they kept sliding off my shoulders so I had to wiggle and shrug to get them back into position. Eventually Kansas asked what was the matter with me, so I told her. She didn't make a big deal of it other than telling me all she ever wears is a sports bra because it's practical, comfortable, never shifts and the straps don't dig in. She pulled a wide strap out from under her T-shirt and let it go with a soft snap to illustrate her point. I went home and told Mom I wanted a sports bra and she said, "What for?" She said I didn't need the support and it would only flatten me (which didn't sound like such a bad idea actually), and that the one she'd bought me was much prettier. I told her it wasn't any good for equestrian athletes like me and Kansas and she hasn't mentioned it since.

On normal days, when my dad hasn't been possessed by his shadow side, I ride my bike to school and go the long way that takes me past the stable. If I time it right I can say good morning to Brooklyn as Kansas leads him out to his paddock. I could say good morning to Kansas too of course, but I usually forget, and it doesn't bother Kansas at all because we're both members of the herd of horsewomen, so she understands. Kansas is wonderful. She is totally not normal in the best sort of way.

Today, since I'm walking and I'm short of time, I have to take a more direct route to school. This means I have to sneak through the middle of our subdivision where all the other kids walk, which is another reason I prefer the long route.

I'm about halfway to school, thinking maybe by some fluke I could still elude my tormentors, when I hear loud footsteps and panting coming up fast behind me. I steel myself, and hold tight to the straps of my backpack, expecting it to be ripped from my shoulders as Amber flies past. I can't believe my ears when I hear, "Hey, Sylvia! Wait up!"

It's Logan Losino.

He staggers to a walk beside me, puffing hard and trying not to show it.

"I never see you walking to school," he says.

"My dad drove over my bike with his Explorer," I say. Usually I have trouble talking to Logan Losino, but today seems different, maybe because I dreamt about him last night. Maybe because I'm still disturbed by my dad's behaviour and could use an ally.

"Bummer," says Logan. "How did he do that?"

"He must have had it in four-wheel drive," I say.

Logan laughs as though I've told him a joke. Logan is always laughing and joking around. Usually I don't mind, and any other day I'd be thrilled about Logan thinking I was a jokester like him. But right now I'd prefer my problems were taken more seriously.

"I've never seen my dad so mad at me," I say. I don't add anything about how he threw my bike across the yard in case Logan thinks this is an issue for Child Protection Services. I don't want my dad to get into trouble. Or at least not that much trouble.

"Do you think you'll be walking to school from now on?" says Logan. He sounds way too happy, as though he's nowhere near seeing this tragedy from my point of view.

So I tell him that it's very depressing for me, and that the worst part is that I can't ride my bike to see my horse after class, which seems like pretty severe punishment for a small oversight.

Logan chews on his lip to fight back a smile. Nice friend.

We walk in silence for half a block. When we reach the corner, Logan points to a small house down the street. "See that one, with the boat parked in the yard? That's where Amber and Topaz live."

Amber and Topaz are twins, but they're not identical so as far as I'm concerned they're no big deal. From my perspective there's an advantage to them not being identical, because they have different interests. When they first moved to town last year, both of them tormented me full-time. Since Topaz found out that I'm into horses, she's been nicer to me and only torments me half the time. Amber is still relentless, and sometimes Topaz will get her off my case. If she doesn't, Logan Losino is often mysteriously available to come to my rescue.

I discover that I've stopped, and am staring at the front door of Amber and Topaz's house, expecting them to launch themselves in my direction at any second. I still haven't fully recovered from being attacked by my dad, so I don't know if I can cope with Amber and Topaz. I wish I'd taken a mental health day for myself.

"It's early, they probably haven't left yet. If we keep going we can get to school ahead of them and foil their evil plans," says Logan. He takes my hand and tugs. When he touches me I almost jump out of my skin. "Come on!" he says, laughing.

And I'm running down the street, holding hands with Logan Losino.

I'm holding hands with a boy.

It feels nice, like it did in my dream. It's like a new world opening up for me. I don't know if I'm more excited or anxious, which is a lot like I felt when I got my first horse, but at least there I had my Pony Club manual to back me up.

# chapter
## three

I see my cousin Taylor in the cafeteria at lunch, surrounded by her extensive fan club. She was popular last year, but now that she's an amputee it's become ridiculous. I find this very confusing. There is Taylor, missing a digit and her popularity has soared, while I'm missing a whole X chromosome, and have to eat lunch all by myself.

Taylor waves me over, which is nice, considering I'm younger, a grade behind her, and a social leper. The fan club looks at me with disinterest and drifts away to another table. I hear them talking about vampires and werewolves. There's another movie out apparently. I don't understand all the interest in scary imaginary creatures. I saw a werewolf movie once and it was stupid, and hardly scary at all.

I take a vacated seat beside Taylor.

"My mom's picking me up after school and she's going to drop me at the barn so I can spend some time with Spike," says Taylor. "We could throw your bike in the back if you want a lift."

"I don't have my bike. My dad ran over it this morning—I left it in the wrong place and he didn't notice. I have to walk straight home."

"Well, Cookie," says Taylor, doing a good job of mimicking my mom, "sooner or later you do have to understand that there are consequences for your behaviour."

I look away, because I don't like anyone but me criticizing my mom, and see Amber across the cafeteria, closing in on us like a heat-seeking missile. Amber idolizes my cousin. I turn back to Taylor so I don't have to watch Amber approach. "My mom wasn't too bad. She was going to drive me to school but Dad wouldn't let her."

"*He wouldn't let her?*" repeats Taylor. "Your mom went along with that? My mom should have another talk with her."

"Oh no," I say in a panic. My dad thinks Auntie Sally is a lunatic, and makes a point of not agreeing with anything she says. "My mom said he was just giving in to his shadow side, and we can sort it out when his mood is better."

Taylor snorts. "My mom says women shouldn't let men get away with stuff like that. She says it's a form of bullying."

"Your mom is divorced," I remind her, and when she shrugs I say, "Twice. Plus she can't keep a boyfriend." This is something my dad says about Auntie Sally, and now that I've quoted him I feel badly, because I've criticized Taylor's mom.

Taylor doesn't seem to mind. "She could have a boyfriend if she wanted to," she says. "These days she says that men can be handy to have around, but for the most part they're more trouble than they're worth."

Amber plunks her tray on the table across from us. "Hi Taylor, hi Sylvia. Mind if I join you?"

Amber never calls me Sylvia. She has a whole zoo-full of names she prefers for me, though apparently not while Taylor is around to be impressed. She takes a seat without waiting for an answer, folds her arms on the table and leans over them, so her chest bulges out even more obviously than usual. I try not to look, but it's as though she's asking me to. If I develop like this after I start taking estrogen, I'm going to wear a flattening sports bra all the time.

Taylor flashes her a polite smile. "Sorry, Amber, we're discussing a family problem."

Amber's cheeks pinken. She's used to getting her way. Taylor doesn't back down.

Amber makes a show of suddenly noticing that Topaz is sitting at another table, then picks up her tray and cruises away as though this was her idea, as though she hadn't just been rejected in full view of everyone in the cafeteria. I could almost feel sorry for her if she wasn't such a faker. Topaz doesn't look that happy to see her either. Amber makes her move her chair, then takes over the conversation with her usual arm-waving theatrics.

"Besides," says Taylor, "my mom loves bugging your dad." She's picked up the conversation right where we left off. She's dealt with Amber with hardly a thought, flicking her off like she was no more than a piece of lint. I couldn't do that in a million years; Amber would stomp me if I tried.

Maybe if I wasn't an only child, I'd have better social skills. Taylor has had lots of practice over the years with her sisters. Her younger sister Erika is a total immature crybaby, and her older sister Stephanie is the most pushy person I know and fortunately now away at university.

Taylor is crushing her empty milk carton with her elbow and looking around the cafeteria for her entourage. I guess I should have been talking more instead of losing myself in thought. I hate trying to make conversation, and I'm not very good at it. But I don't want to sit alone, I don't want Taylor to leave, so I'm scrambling for possible topics when I feel a large shape looming behind me, then Franko kicks out the chair on the other side of Taylor and perches his great bulk on the edge of it.

Franko is Taylor's boyfriend, though I've never understood why. She's so pretty and popular she could go out with any superstar she wants, and instead she's picked Franko. He's Logan Losino's older brother, which is about the only good thing he has going for him in my opinion.

"Hey Babe," he says. He drops his gym bag at his feet and boots it under the lunch table.

A scent envelops us. It's sharp and medicinal, like the liniment Kansas uses on the horses when she thinks their muscles are sore. I wonder at first if the smell is coming from the gym bag, but then I notice that any time Franko moves, the scent grows stronger, wafting at me in waves of warm air.

I haven't seen Franko for a while. Of course our paths tend not to cross—he's in grade twelve. Again. Last year he was away somewhere so I saw him even less. I didn't even know he and Taylor were dating until a few months ago. I don't see him much this year either because when he's not in class Taylor says he's either playing football or working out in the gym.

Franko doesn't acknowledge me. It's as though I don't exist, or I'm invisible, which is okay in a way because I have to admit that Franko scares me. I've never spoken to him. Being around him makes my tongue seize up.

Franko whispers something in Taylor's ear and she giggles.

Ugh. I would leave if I had anywhere else to go, but the cafeteria is packed, there's not a single empty table. I unwrap my sandwich and take a bite. I try to stay tucked in out of sight behind Taylor, but then Franko leans forward and props an elbow on the lunch table. He's wearing a sleeveless shirt with big loopy armholes to show off the muscles on his muscles. Usually he reminds me of a frog: he's got no neck and his arms don't fold neatly against his body like they're supposed to, plus his hands look puny in relation to the rest of him.

He slides his elbow forward so he sprawls across the table. I can see a big wodge of black hair, like someone's cut a patch out of a bear pelt and stuffed it into Franko's armpit. If nothing else, Franko's good at growing hair. He grows more beard than my dad—I can see little black pinpricks all over his face where he's shaved. Taylor has told me she makes him shave every day, otherwise he has a scratchy growth that gives her whisker burn when they kiss. Sometimes this happens anyway and Taylor says that it feels like her face has been removed with sandpaper. I don't see the appeal. Taylor, meanwhile, has sort of melted into her chair, nodding and smiling at everything he says. Where has her IQ gone?

I sit there in my own isolated universe, and all in all it doesn't seem fair that Taylor has a million friends, and a boyfriend (such as he is), plus she can go to the stable to see Spike after school while I have to walk home—alone. I feel so irked, so much on the outside of things, so tired of this, that I do the unthinkable. I speak. In front of Franko.

"Hey, Taylor, you're sure I can have a ride after school?" I say.

"Of course I'm sure." She doesn't look at me, her eyes are glued on Franko.

Franko looks past Taylor in my direction, as though surprised to hear a voice and needing to figure out where it came from. He finds me. His eye lashes are thick and dark, and his eyes a deep soft brown.

Okay. I get it. There's one attraction—he has great eyes.

I'm not worth much attention though; his focus immediately slides back to Taylor.

"You're going out to see your mule this afternoon?" he says. "I thought you were going to watch us practice."

"He's not a mule. He's a hinny," Taylor corrects him gently, though I'm sure she's explained this a thousand times before.

"Gonna do some more animal communicating?" says Franko. His tone is mocking.

I'm not impressed, but no one's asking me.

When Taylor doesn't answer, Franko says, "Let's get out of here." He grabs his gym bag then slips his other arm around her waist and helps her to her feet, not that she needs the assistance—I know her balance is fine as long as she's not doing something fancy like trying to stand on pointe. His fingers disappear up under her shirt. Taylor places her hand on his forearm and calmly pushes his arm down.

I think about Logan taking my hand. What if he wanted to do something like this instead? Would I know what to do?

Franko meanwhile is acting hurt and innocent. "What?" he says, sliding his hand back up under her shirt.

"Franko," says Taylor evenly. She uses a totally neutral tone of voice and expression on her face, like I've seen Kansas do when she's training the horses or her new puppy Bernadette. Maybe that's it. Maybe dealing with boys is just like animal training.

Taylor retrieves Franko's hand and clasps it firmly, lacing her delicate fingers through his thick lumpy ones. She doesn't say anything else. I guess she doesn't want to reprimand him in public, not even in front of invisible me. She's told me before that Franko is sensitive and his feelings are hurt easily. I'll have to take her word for it. Taylor has also told me that she is grateful to him for standing by her after her accident. She said that another boy might have dumped her after she lost her toe and became deformed. From what I can tell there are other parts of Taylor's anatomy that are of much greater importance to Franko than a missing toe.

Franko shifts his grip on his gym bag, and that's when I notice his name embossed on the side, and boy do I feel stupid. I've made another ridiculous spelling mistake, something I'm famous for. Franko's name isn't Franko. It's Franco. For months and months I've been thinking of him as Franko, and it's stupid but the change in spelling instantly makes my feelings about him change too. Franco is softer than Franko. Maybe Taylor has known this all along—that underneath all the macho muscle there is a gentle kind person.

Why does life have to be so confusing? Why can't we all have labels that say "Good Person" or "Bad Person"? It would make everything so much simpler.

"See you later, Sylvia," says Taylor over her shoulder as Franco drags her away, leaving nothing behind but his smell, which I have to say is still the only thing I really like about him, and only because it reminds me of horses.

I hunch over my tray and finish eating my lunch, hoping that Amber (Bad Person) doesn't notice I've been cut from the herd and am sitting there all alone and vulnerable.

# chapter
## four

I'm late leaving school because Mr. Brumby makes me stay behind so he can explain one more time where I am going wrong with my math problems. Afterwards the halls are mercifully near-empty and I make the mistake of letting down my guard. I'm reaching into the back of my locker for my jacket and don't see Amber coming until it's too late. She gives me a two-handed shove as though she's trying to stuff me inside my locker, but I shove back.

"Oh, feisty little monkey," she says, laughing.

Topaz is behind her. "Leave her alone, Amber," she says.

"I wasn't doing anything, it was an accident—I tripped," says Amber, who staggers away down the hallway like a drunk.

Topaz stops beside me. "Sorry," she says.

"You don't need to apologize," I say. "It's Amber who hates me."

"You shouldn't take it personally. She always does this, finds someone to pick on then mounts a campaign against them. She did it at our last school, to a girl who dated her boyfriend before Amber stole him away. Mom made her promise not to do it here. I'm supposed to keep an eye on her and report back, like that would be worth my life."

I can't believe that Topaz is talking to me, let alone ratting out her twin sister. I've never thought of how awful it would be for her to be yoked to someone like Amber for life.

She fully opens my locker door to look at the photo of Brooklyn I have taped inside. "This your horse?"

I tell her yes.

"He's awesome. What's his breeding? Is he a Danish Warmblood? He looks like Blue Matiné—you know, the horse Andreas Helgstrand rode at the World Equestrian Games."

"You think?" Is she teasing me now? Or is she just stupid? Other than being grey, I don't think Brooklyn looks anything at all like Blue Hors Matiné. "He's from Saskatchewan," I tell her, closing my locker door. Despite her disclosure, despite feeling begrudgingly impressed that Topaz knows about Matiné who I have seen on YouTube and adore, I don't want Topaz looking at Brooklyn.

"Oh well, whatever," she says, and bolts off because Amber is shouting for her at the end of the hallway.

I stuff my books in my backpack and slowly follow them to the door. I check through the window before I open it. They're standing at the bottom step with Logan Losino. Logan is kidding around with them but keeping an eye on the door. I should be safe enough with him around, especially if I maintain my momentum. Kansas tells me during my riding lessons that when in doubt, go forward. I think that's because horses can be more troublesome if they're going too slow. They can get their heads down and buck you off, or they can spook or become distracted. So it's worth a try when dealing with the little animals in the schoolyard.

I burst out the doorway and jog down the steps. Logan Losino moves into my path, hampering my brilliant plan. "Walking home?" he says.

"You want to walk home with *her?*" says Amber.

I hear a car honk from the parking lot, and turn to see Auntie Sally waving and shouting for me.

"I have a ride," I say to Logan, and because he suddenly looks so sad I add, "I'm going to the barn to see my horse."

Amber says, "Hey Logan, you can walk home with me, and I won't hold you back like shorty-pants the pygmy chimp."

Logan ignores her.

"As a matter of fact, I won't hold you back at all," says Amber, wiggling her eyebrows.

Logan still pays her no attention. "Maybe I could come with you to the barn some time," he says to me.

I'm so dumbfounded I can't even think. "Sure, if you want," I say, then I tell him I have to go, and I dash for the car. Why on earth would Logan Losino want to come to the barn? There'd be nothing for him to do. He'd have to hang around while I groomed Brooklyn and rode for an hour, then groomed again and maybe cleaned up the stall a little. It would be totally boring. Unless Logan likes horses, which seems pretty doubtful.

As we pull out of the parking lot I see that Amber has jumped on Logan's back and is riding him, pretending he's a race horse. Her arm is going up and down as though she's whipping him to go faster. Logan is laughing and breaks into a canter as Amber leans around and I'm pretty sure she sticks her tongue in his ear. Disgusting. I don't know how he stands her.

"How was school, Sylvie?" says Auntie Sally, turning around to look at me in the back seat and almost clipping a car parked at the side of the road.

"Mom! Pay attention!" says Taylor from the passenger seat.

"Taylor tells me your dad is on the rampage," says

Auntie Sally. "I'll have to have a word with your mom the marriage therapist again."

"Oh I don't think so, Auntie Sally, we should wait until—"

"Your mom may have lots of university education, but frankly it's all theory, and with only one marriage under her belt there are some things about men she just won't understand."

Taylor swings around to look at me. "I'm going to practice some new animal communication techniques with Spike today. I've been reading a book that says if I go into a kind of meditative trance while standing beside him, and keep my mind blank, I can pick up his thoughts."

I look from one of them to the other. In profile, they show the identical angle where their noses meet their foreheads. They think the same too. They are both so certain about what they know. I wish I could be like that. I wish I could know things with certainty instead of being unsure about almost everything. Why couldn't I have inherited that gene?

# chapter
## five

Kansas isn't at the barn when Auntie Sally drops us off. Her truck is in the parking lot, all her horses are present and accounted for, but her dog Bernadette is missing too. My guess is that they've gone for a walk.

Taylor has a different idea. "I bet Declan picked them up. I bet they're on a hot date."

It's difficult for me to imagine Kansas on a hot date, but Taylor knows more about this sort of thing than I do (granted, that isn't saying much) so I guess she's right. Declan is our farrier. He does all our horse shoeing. He doesn't talk much and he wears T-shirts that are too small and Kansas goes silly whenever he's around.

Kansas used to be very attentive and supportive whenever I saw her, but then she met Declan, and then she adopted Bernadette. Fortunately she taught me a lot before she became distracted, so I am competent around the horses and don't need her all the time.

Taylor could use more guidance (particularly around Spike's biting issues), even though she never actually rides him. She's much more interested in developing a "relationship" with him. Taylor says Kansas actually interferes with this because she has so many conventional horse-training ideas. Taylor says Kansas's consciousness needs to be raised. I don't know what she's talking about. I think Kansas is brilliant and if her consciousness were any higher she'd be living on the space station.

I leave Taylor to commune with Spike and I tack up Brooklyn.

Brooklyn is fourteen hands and he looks like a little war-horse. He thinks he's one too. Kansas figures he's part Andalusian or maybe Kiger Mustang but we'll never know for sure because the previous owner is in an extended-care facility and he's got dementia even worse than my grandpa (which is saying something) so he can't remember which of his horses came from where and no one can find any registration papers.

Not that I care.

I ride Brooklyn around the ring a few times, but it gets boring. Kansas doesn't like me jumping on my own, she says it's too dangerous, and what if something happened, dot dot dot? Not that anything would happen. Brooklyn takes care of me. He's an excellent horse.

I put Brooklyn on a loose rein and let him wander where he wants to go. He heads to the out-gate and I think, what the heck? I lean over, spring the latch, then grab the top bar of the gate and urge Brooklyn forward. As though he's reading my mind, when the gate swings open Brooklyn walks through and pivots so I can keep my hand on the rail the whole time and slam it shut, exactly like the pros I see in trail class competitions on YouTube. I can hardly believe it, because we've never practiced this sort of thing. I pat his neck and tell him he's a very good boy. I love this horse. He is so smart.

I leave Brooklyn on a loose rein. I want to see where he'll decide to go. Kansas has taken me on some trail rides where she rode Hambone and I rode her lesson pony Electra. Kansas wanted me to spend the first month or two on Brooklyn in the ring to be sure we knew each other before heading out on the trails. It's been over a month now, and Brooklyn and I are like soul mates, but Kansas has been too busy for trail rides. Too busy with Declan. Too busy with Bernadette.

Brooklyn takes the trail up the outside of the paddock and across the unfenced field beside Kansas's property. His ears are perked forward and his steps are quick. He's happy to be out of the ring. So am I.

I straighten my helmet on my head. It's a bit looser than it should be since I carved out a piece of the liner. I did this in the summer, when I was taking the growth hormone, and fell off my bike, and ended up with a lump in the middle of my forehead. For a while I wondered if I was growing a horn like a unicorn. I had a dream that Logan Losino grew a horn too, so it really freaked me out the first day of school when he was wearing that silly cap pulled down over his forehead. I have a very fertile imagination. Or I did until recently. I'm more mature now. From now on I have resolved to be logical whenever possible, and not get carried away with fanciful ideas. This should make life a lot easier for me.

I say, "Brooklyn, you can trot if you want." He picks up a trot. I shorten the reins slightly, and look over my shoulder in case Kansas has appeared back at the barn. She'd be upset if she saw me trotting off alone towards the woods. So would my parents. Too bad.

Besides, I'm not alone. I'm with Brooklyn.

I love being in the woods. It's better than hiking, because I'm higher up, so I can see above the undergrowth. I don't need to be afraid of anything, because Brooklyn can outrun a dog. Or a bear. Or a man. Thinking about all the things that might need to be outrun frightens me a little. I need a joke to bring me back to normal, so I tell myself that Brooklyn could also outrun a non-identical twin, which makes me laugh out loud.

Brooklyn hears me laughing and picks up the pace, then breaks into a canter. This is fun! There's a small tree down across the path, and he jumps it like it's nothing. Wow. We're riding cross-country. This is exactly what I used to do in my lucid dreams, except this is real. Boy oh boy.

We round a corner and there's some great crashing noise in the woods. Brooklyn bounces a big stride sideways and stops. I barely manage to stay in the middle of the saddle and not land up on his neck. Brooklyn stares into the woods. A deer stares back at us. Brooklyn figures this out the same time I do and launches himself back onto the path at a trot. He's having as much fun as I am.

We come to a fork in the path. When I'm out with Kansas she takes the left branch which circles around back to the barn. Brooklyn opts for the right one. Virgin territory. Ha ha again. A virgin on virgin territory. Double virgins. Triple if you count Brooklyn who is a gelding and in all likelihood a virgin too. I'm definitely turning into a jokester, just like Logan Losino.

Brooklyn lengthens his trot so it feels like we're flying. Tears stream out of my eyes we're moving so fast. The footing is perfect and cushions every footfall. We round a bend, plunge down a short hill, and suddenly we're at the river.

Brooklyn stops. We both study the water bubbling and gurgling around an expanse of exposed boulders. Brooklyn takes a few tentative steps into the melee until all four feet are in the water. He is such a keener. We will be an unbeatable team when it comes time for competing cross-country. I sit back so I interfere as little as possible with his balance, and that's when I see the huge animal beside the far river bank.

# chapter
## six

Between the sounds of the rushing water, and the muffling of Brooklyn's hoofsteps in the soft ground, the animal hasn't heard us.

At first I think the obvious. This is a bear. A large bear, huddled in the water, fishing maybe. Except it's not black enough. We only have black bears here, no brown ones, no grizzlies.

Brooklyn sees it too. His body tenses, and then I feel his heart pounding right through the saddle. Holy crap. He raises his head and blows a trumpet call out his nose, sounding like a bull elephant.

The creature leaps straight up in the air, exactly like I saw the werewolves do in that movie, with incredible strength. When he lands, he crouches in the water and turns to look at us. He doesn't swivel his head on his neck like we would, but twists his shoulders to bring us into view. He's at least twenty metres away, so I can't see him with absolute clarity, and I only have a few seconds before he turns away, but I sure don't think he has a werewolf face. Was I imagining? Because it almost looked more like a monkey face, on a head with no neck, kind of like Franco but even more so. If not a werewolf, then what kind of bear would this be?

The creature wades smoothly out of the boulder-strewn river. He bounds gracefully up the bank and stops and turns his whole body and looks at us again. I notice something else: he isn't a he. He's a she, with large hairy breasts. I've watched a lot of Animal Planet and National Geographic, and I've never seen a bear with breasts before. It makes me feel sick, as though I'm seeing something I'm not supposed to see, or possibly something that isn't supposed to exist. I want to be logical and I don't want my imagination to become overactive again, but seeing this creature makes me think that I'd be much better off if a unicorn leapt out of the bush and sprinkled us with fairy dust.

Brooklyn blows another elephant call; the creature steps effortlessly over a fallen tree then walks into the woods and disappears. On her hind legs. Not like a bear at all.

Immediately it's as though she was never there, as though I imagined everything. Except that Brooklyn is still vibrating beneath me. He trumpets yet another challenge. I give him a squeeze with my legs as a request to return his focus to me, and gently urge him to bring his head around so we can turn and get back home. He is only too eager to oblige, and takes off at a gallop out of the water. He has surprised me, so I'm not in balance and for a moment it's all I can do to hang on and avoid low-hanging branches as we head up the path. He grunts beneath me, pushing for speed, pushing for home.

I tell him to whoa. He ignores me. This has never happened before. I take a grip on the reins and pull. If anything he goes faster.

I'm on a runaway!

I wonder if he's going too fast to make the corner where

the trail branches, whether the soft footing will give way and leave us sprawled in a heap, with me on the bottom, where my grieving parents will find my body some days from now. They will never forgive Kansas. My dad will kill her after he's finished killing Brooklyn, and then he'll spend the rest of his life in prison, leaving my mom all alone with only Auntie Sally and her memories to comfort her.

Somehow I recall Kansas talking to me about using a pulley rein to stop in emergencies. We never practiced it much because she said it was too hard on the horse. We're quickly coming up on the fork in the trail. I try to remember what Kansas taught me. I grab some mane in my right hand along with the rein and hold tight. I slide my left hand forward on the other rein, take hold and pull up and back with all my might.

Brooklyn bounces to a jagged trot, and finally he walks. He's quivering and sweaty and I vault off because he feels like he's ready to misinterpret the least movement from my seat as a cue to explode into another gallop. I flip the reins over his head and tell him he has to walk. Maybe by the time we reach the barn he will have cooled off and no one will suspect what we've been up to.

He prances beside me.

He's not frightened. He's excited. He's been having the time of his life. There's a whole other side to steady dependable Brooklyn that I never encountered in the riding ring.

We take the fork that will lead us most directly back to the barn. I figure I have about twenty minutes of walking time to put together a plausible story about what I've been up to which will stop me from being in deep trouble with my parents and with Kansas. We're about a hundred metres along, and I've come up with exactly nothing when ahead

I see Taylor, walking beside Spike. Taylor is chattering away like a little bird and doesn't notice me at first though Spike's ears wobble into an upright position when he catches sight of his pal Brooklyn.

I take a deep breath. There are so many things I have to avoid talking about. For the sake of my sanity, there are also things I need to avoid even thinking about. I was trail riding by myself, and I know better and I shouldn't have. My easy-going reliable horse ran away with me and I barely managed to bring him under control with an emergency pulley rein stop. But the most difficult thing is that I saw something unimaginable. That's the part I don't want to think about. My brain folds in on itself any time I retrieve the memory of that creature. How can I possibly explain any of this to Taylor? I will never be able to find the right words.

As it turns out, I needn't have worried. Taylor is busy in the psychic world and out of touch with the perilous planet we are actually occupying.

"Oh this is where you got to," she says. "We had a feeling you'd be here. I've been communicating with Spike and he told me to come this way."

They are blocking the path to home. Spike has his usual semi-annoyed look, his great ears half-cocked. He nuzzles Taylor's pocket then grabs a bit of fabric with his teeth (something I'd never let Brooklyn get away with). "Okay, you were right," she tells him. "There's your reward." She gives him half a carrot.

"It's getting late, we should probably head back," I tell her.

"Oh sure." She turns Spike halfway around and he plants himself crosswise on the trail, sniffing the air in the direction of the river. His ears point forward. He stomps a front foot.

Taylor places a hand on his neck and closes her eyes for a moment. When she's done communicating she turns and translates for me. "Stinky dog, he says. Over and over. Stinky dog stinky dog stinky dog."

Some dog, I think, but I'm not about to correct him. I just want to get out of here.

Spike stomps his foot again. Taylor gives him a pat, then tugs on the lead rope. Spike ignores her. Taylor pulls on the rope as hard as she can and Spike braces against it, staring steadfast to the river. I figure we're stuck here forever, where we can be breakfast lunch and dinner for the hairy monster and her family, but then Brooklyn reaches forward and head-butts Spike on his hip, knocking him sufficiently off balance for Taylor to get the front end moving back onto the path where they walk happily in the direction of the barn. And safety.

"Did you go for a swim?" she calls over her shoulder. "Brooklyn looks kind of wet." She hasn't noticed that he's also breathing hard.

I can't tell her what really happened. If it gets back to my parents I'll never be allowed to ride again.

"It was deeper than I thought," I say.

"Silly goose," says Taylor. She scratches Spike between his ears then loops her arm over his withers, the lead rope slack in her other hand. "Animal communication is easier than I thought. I bet I could teach it to you."

Is she not even going to ask why I'm on foot and not riding?

"I know you don't think of yourself as being very spiritual, but I think all of us are born psychic, then most people forget. It's kind of a mass psychic amnesia."

I wouldn't mind a little amnesia right now. I keep seeing in my mind the image of that creature's face and it freaks me out and makes me feel sick again. I've seen something I shouldn't. I can't make sense of it. It's almost like the time that Taylor and I were trying to haul Bunga out from under Auntie Sally's bed so we could clip his toenails and we found her vibrator, and I thought it was some special kind of curling iron so Taylor had to explain it to me so then on top of feeling mortified and embarrassed I also felt really stupid. I had to work hard at not imagining Auntie Sally with a sex toy. Which is probably what I should do now: I should work hard at not picturing that creature. I should tell myself I just imagined it.

"Spike says to tell you that you don't need to be frightened, because he will protect us," says Taylor.

I draw in a breath then slide my fingers up under Brooklyn's mane and hang onto the crest of his neck. "What would I be frightened of? Animal communication?" There's a sneer in my voice that reminds me of Franco, and I'm not proud of it. Taylor is, after all, trying to be helpful.

"I'm just telling you what he said," says Taylor. "Spike is very intuitive. Plus donkeys and hinnies and mules are used as livestock protection animals. I've seen a video on YouTube where a mule kills a cougar."

There are some crashing sounds from the bushes, then a deer bounds across the trail ahead of us. I break out in a fresh sweat. The deer is nothing to be frightened of, but what if something was chasing it? Something tall and hairy that moves with the grace of a werewolf and has the face of an ape? Have I discovered a were-ape?

Taylor is humming. Taylor who is usually afraid of everything, and here she is in the woods with wild animals all around us and she's contented and relaxed and totally oblivious.

"Sing with me," she says. "Let's do *Sound of Music* songs." She launches into the title track.

I don't want to sing, especially not *Sound of Music* songs. I'm not retro like Taylor but it occurs to me that the more noise we make, the better chance there is of scaring off the unclassified wildlife. So I draw a deep breath and join her, and when I can't remember the words I la-la-la as loud as I can. Taylor stops singing and looks back over her shoulder at us, then carries on with another verse.

When we reach the barn, Auntie Sally is waiting for us. She's sitting in her car reading a home decorating magazine.

"We went for a walk," explains Taylor. Then, almost as if she knows something is going on and wants to distract Auntie Sally, she says, "You know, Mom, Sylvia can really sing. She has a voice like yours once she gets going, with bells in it."

Auntie Sally is pleased with this news, and launches into the history of her singing career, unfortunately sidelined by motherhood, and how lessons really help when you have raw talent which sadly none of her own girls inherited. I don't argue with her at all, or tell her I have no time for singing lessons. I'm just glad that Auntie Sally is so perfectly happy to ignore the fact that Brooklyn is fully tacked-up with bridle and saddle. There will be no news bulletin going to my parents about my doing a solo trail ride. Brooklyn has cooled enough that I give him a quick brush-over then leave him in his paddock. Fortunately Kansas is still nowhere to be found—she wouldn't have been as easily fooled.

It's a miracle, but I've escaped getting into trouble. Except for the trouble that I'm in with myself, trying to control my brain and the image that I can't erase.

# chapter
## seven

Dad is in a better mood after work, which is not to say great. At least he's not throwing things. He even volunteers to take me to the bike shop in the morning to talk to them about fixing my bike.

"Fixing it?" says Mom.

"It just needs a little straightening. It's a perfectly good bike," says Dad.

"It's a perfectly good twisted metal sculpture," says Mom.

I hate it when this happens, when something I've done becomes the focus of one of my parents' arguments. Though even if I wasn't around, they'd have lots to disagree about, they wouldn't exactly go back to being a happy romantic couple. They are always disagreeing on money for one thing. Dad says it's what comes of him being a saver who's married a spender. Mom says it's what comes from her marrying a total cheapskate. It usually gets worse from there.

I don't have a great appetite at dinner. As much as I try not to, I can't stop thinking about the big hairy creature with the big hairy breasts. I'm pushing the peas around on my plate hoping no one will notice that I'm not eating. Fat chance. My mom is always on the lookout for my developing an eating disorder.

"Eat up, Pumpkin," she says. "There's fruit salad for dessert."

I eat a pea. Mom reaches over and feels my forehead. I force myself to swallow a chunk of potato before she comes up with some sort of terminal diagnosis requiring quarantine in the house.

"How was school?" she asks.

School. That was like an ice age ago. I try to remember, then give up and tell her it was fine.

"Maybe she's tired out from walking to school and back," says Dad with a smug tone that makes me squirm.

No one was home when Auntie Sally dropped me off. She promised not to tell.

"Yeah, that's it," I say, steadying myself. "I'm not used to walking."

"It's a good lesson for you then," says Dad, tipping his head sagely.

Oh brother. But I nod. "That's right, Dad." I'll say anything that helps me get my bike back so I can spend time with Brooklyn and Kansas. Not that I can talk to Kansas about what I saw in the woods; she'd kill me for going off on my own like that. I wish there was someone I could talk to, and for some reason I think of Logan Losino and feel better. I'm even able to finish my dinner, then I go to my bedroom to do my homework. It's Friday night and I have all weekend to finish it, but I'd rather keep Saturday and Sunday free for riding. Or bike shopping. Sigh.

I don't sleep very well that night. I don't have any lucid dreams either.

In the morning Dad and I head out to the bike store.

He has a tee-time at the golf course at eleven, so he figures he has enough time if we stay organized and focused.

He's in a pretty good mood when we set out. More like his normal mood. Normally my dad is a fairly happy guy who jokes around a lot. He can get uptight about money, but he makes his living as a financial planner and advisor, so I guess that makes sense. Kind of like how Mom is a mental health professional and always terrified I'm showing the signs of some mental illness, while Dad is looking for signs of poor financial management which would lead us to financial ruin and living in a cardboard box in a ditch. I guess when you're sufficiently afraid of something, there are signs of it all over the place.

We hit every red light on the way into town and I can feel Dad's mood deteriorating with each delay. We reach Fifth Street, and ahead of us someone is trying to parallel park a van outside Graham's Jewelry. There's steady traffic coming the other direction and no way around.

Dad checks his watch and drums the steering wheel with his thumbs. The rear wheel of the van hits the curb and then it draws ahead into the traffic lane again.

"Second time lucky," I say, trying to lighten the atmosphere. The van backs towards the space again, but ends up about six feet away from the curb. The driver pulls ahead into the lane.

"Jesus Christ," says Dad.

I look behind us. There are at least five cars waiting now.

"Moron!" shouts Dad as the van ends up in the curb again. "Some people don't deserve to drive."

I turn on the car radio, thinking the distraction might help, but Dad switches it off. He throws the transmission into park and flings open his door. I shrink down in my seat. What's he going to do?

Dad walks up to the driver door of the van and opens it. I see him gesture for the driver to get out. She's a girl I recognize from school—a member of Taylor's vast fan club. Dad points to the sidewalk and she goes and stands there. He climbs in behind the wheel of the van, drives ahead until it's straight, then backs into the parking spot, perfectly, first time. He gets out of the van, slams the door, and stomps back to our SUV. I'm so embarrassed I could die. I try to sink lower in my seat. I hope the girl on the sidewalk doesn't see me and spread the news around school about what a total Neanderthal my dad is. If Amber hears this story, I'm dead.

Dad opens his car door. That's when I hear the applause. I raise my head enough to see out my window. There are people on the sidewalk clapping and whistling. Dad's face transforms from glowering storm clouds to happy entertainer. He pauses and bows to the crowd, then climbs back into his driver's seat. He guns the engine and the wheels squeal on the pavement, almost as though he's showing off, like a sixteen-year-old. I can't believe it.

Fortunately there's a parking space for us right in front of the bike shop. Dad hauls the twisted wreckage of my bike out of the back of the SUV. He has to carry it into the shop because none of the wheels are working.

The guy in the bike store tries not to laugh when my dad asks him how much it would cost to straighten the frame; he covers his face with the inside of his elbow and pretends to cough, but I can tell he's faking even before he winks at me. Dad doesn't notice—he's too busy trying to get the warp out of the front wheel with his bare hands.

"I'm afraid this is one for the recycle bin," says the bike guy. "I can give you a good deal on another bike though. We have a couple of smaller-framed models on sale right now."

"On sale?" says Dad. He's heard the magic words.

"Twenty-percent off," says the bike guy.

"With full warranty?" says Dad.

"The warranty wouldn't cover everything. Just manufacturer's defects. Not traffic accidents." He winks at me again, but Dad doesn't see.

"Whatever," says Dad.

The guy pulls a pink and white bike out of the rack. Oh no.

"I'm fourteen," I tell him, which obviously confuses him and he's about to turn to Dad so I say, "I know I don't look it. I'm short for my age." I point at the pink monstrosity. "This is a bike for a six-year old."

Dad says, "I think you should try it, Munchkin. It looks like it'll fit you."

"We have a small frame in blue," says the clerk, "but it's not on sale. It'd be another two hundred dollars."

"Two hundred!" says Dad. I see his eyes flick to the clock on the wall. Ten-thirty. There's not much time for negotiation.

The clerk steadies Pinky and I climb on. There are sparkles on the handlebar. He says it fits. Oh god. I hate pink. But it's also my fault that I need a new bike: I parked the old one in the wrong place and that's why Dad drove over it. Plus my horse is expensive and if extra money has to be spent on my behalf, I'd rather it go towards riding.

But *pink*?

"Any room for adjustment when she grows?" Dad asks. He never gives up on this one. He still expects a miracle to occur and maybe overnight some time I will shoot up to five feet tall. The clerk nods and tells us there's lots of room yet. For a growth spurt. Ha!

Dad pulls out his charge card. I close my eyes and

sigh. Okay, I should be grateful, I really should. It could be worse—the bike could have streamers, or training wheels. But I don't know how I'm going to hold my head up at school.

I'm pushing my new pink abomination to the door when something catches Dad's eye. "That's a good looking bike," he says to the clerk.

"Our new road bike. Disk brakes, of course. Alloy frame. Carbon forks."

Dad wraps his fingers around the grips on the handlebar. It's a beautiful bike, all black and silver, exactly like I would have liked.

"Why don't you take it for a spin?" says the clerk.

Dad checks his watch. He stares at the bike. "I haven't ridden a bike since I was a kid." He pauses, thinking. "Must be twenty years…maybe more." It's like he's talking to the air. He isn't really in the room anymore, he's lost in space or lost in his past. Does this make him lost in space-time?

"No kidding," says the bike guy. "You don't look that old."

Somehow this draws Dad's attention back to the room. "Really?" he says.

"You'll notice a lot of improvements. And you could go biking with your daughter."

I glare at the guy. Is he nuts? Hasn't he caused enough trouble for me? I ride my bike for transportation purposes only. I don't have time for recreational rides with my dad. That would cut into my time at the barn.

"Or you could try road racing. There's an active club. Unless you'd prefer a mountain bike, for trails."

Trails? Oh I hope not.

Dad is testing the brake levers, looking wistful. "Maybe I'll come back," he says. He takes a pamphlet with a business card stapled to the top. Then he loads my bike in the SUV and we drive off towards the stable.

"Nice bike," says Dad with a tinge of unfulfilled desire, so I know he's talking about the black one, not mine. "Though maybe if I buy a bike, it should be a trail bike. I could go with you when you're on your horse. We'd have some fun."

I look at him to see if he's serious.

"Oh I'm not so interested in trails any more," I say, which surprises both of us.

"I thought you loved trail riding. I thought you were preparing for riding in cross-country competitions," says Dad.

I shrug. For a change Dad's BlackBerry isn't buzzing him and I have almost his full attention. I wonder if I can trust him. I'd like to know if there are any exotic wild animals in the woods, perhaps escapees from a zoo somewhere, or better still I'd like to know if I was imagining what I saw and hear a logical explanation for it. I watch him as he watches the road. On the other hand, if he thinks I'm in danger on my horse, he'll start treating me like a five-year-old again.

Suddenly his right foot dives for the brake pedal and he swerves the car onto the verge. My seat belt tightens and presses me into the seat cushions. Dad puts a palm on the horn and shouts, "You stupid idiot! Watch where you're going! You can't stop in the middle of the road!" He pulls up on the shoulder beside the other car. There's an old man driving. He's probably the same age as Grandpa. He can barely see over the steering wheel. He's probably not much taller than me, which is amazing but true. "You should have your license revoked!" Dad yells at him.

"Dad," I say, "he's old…"

Dad's face is crimson. He shakes his fist and then, I can't believe it, he gives the guy the finger.

I sink back in my seat. My heart is racing. I'm not used to this. My dad doesn't usually have a bad temper, especially with little old people. What's he going to do next?

He guns the engine, we bounce off down the edge of the road through a mass of pot holes and then lurch back onto the pavement.

"Stupid old fart!" he says.

Obviously this isn't a good time to discuss my trail riding adventures. I'm beginning to think that Dad has enough troubles of his own.

I have to sort out my problems by myself. I can do that. Probably the best thing to do is to focus on ring work for a while, and convince myself that I imagined everything. At worst, I saw a bear, and it ran away. Simple as that.

# chapter
## eight

My simple plan falls apart the minute I set foot in the barn.

Kansas is grooming Hambone in the cross-ties. She wants us to go on a trail ride. Today.

As soon as she tells me this, my ability to convince myself that I imagined everything, or saw a bear, crumbles.

Plus it's too cruelly ironic that I've been dying to do a trail ride for weeks, and Kansas has been saying, "Not yet" or "I don't feel like it," and finally she thinks the time is right and now there's no way I want to go, not with Godzilla out there roaming the woods. How do I get out of this one?

"Couldn't I have a jumping lesson?" I say.

"You want a lesson instead of a trail ride? You are getting keen," says Kansas, and for a second I think my ploy has succeeded, but then she shakes her head. "You've been in the ring too much lately. I am impressed with your dedication to your horsemanship, but it's time to get out on the trail. It'll be good for you and Brooklyn, and good for me too. I could use a kick in the butt to stop feeling like a slug—I don't know what's the matter with me."

Oh this slays me. The fact that Kansas is impressed by my dedication means more to me than anything in the world, and I can't ruin everything by telling her that yesterday I snuck out of the ring against her orders. If I disappoint her, my heart will break. But if I go out on the trail I run the risk of meeting up with that creature. Given some time, I could possibly re-convince myself I'd imagined the whole thing, but if I see it again today there'll be absolutely no fooling myself. I'll spend the rest of my life in terror, hiding in a closet in my bedroom, never leaving for school, or to get married, or have a career. I just know it, because I'm that kind of person. My imagination has gone wild on me before: when I was little I saw a science fiction movie about human-eating monsters from outer space and couldn't sleep properly for weeks.

"Maybe I'll stay here and practice my flatwork," I say.

Kansas comes out from behind Hambone holding a body brush in one hand. As usual she looks like she selects her clothes from the drop-box at the Salvation Army. Nothing fits quite right, the pocket on her shirt is half-torn, and the button at the top of her jeans is either missing or undone. "You want to practice flat work?" She looks at me with amazement, as though I've said I'd prefer to wait in the barn while they're gone and do math puzzles. "What's going on?"

I'm panic-stricken and study the floor hoping for an idea, or a plausible story. I'm not very good at lying to Kansas. I can do it in an emergency. I'm not sure this is one.

Kansas misreads my silence. "Look, Sylvia, it's not unusual for any of us who spend a lot of time schooling in the ring to feel nervous about heading out on the trail. There's a sense of security with riding inside the fence. But there's more to horsemanship than ring riding. You'll be fine. Your seat is secure and Brooklyn is sensible. I have a world of confidence in the pair of you. You don't need to be nervous. Kelly Cleveland's coming too, there will be three of us. It's a perfect opportunity."

I cannot imagine how Kansas and Dr. Cleveland could protect me from a great hairy were-ape monster, but I can't very well say this. I have to face it: I am doomed, there is no way of avoiding participation in this life-threatening event, so I shuffle off to collect Brooklyn from his paddock. I groom him then tack him up, all at dinosaur-speed in the hope that they'll leave without me, but when I finally make my way out to the riding arena, there they are patiently waiting.

I lead Brooklyn to the mounting block, step into the saddle, then do a couple of laps of the ring at walk and trot, hoping that maybe for once Brooklyn will be lame, but I have no such luck.

Dr. Cleveland peers down at me from Braveheart, who is very tall. Actually they are both very tall. I feel like a midget on a Thelwell pony in comparison. With Hambone being on the chunky side, once we penetrate the forest wilderness Brooklyn and I will make the tastiest little morsel out of this group for sure.

Dr. Cleveland's eyes are wide and shining and Braveheart is making funny snorkeling noises out his nose. He's grinding on the bit with his teeth as much as the snug noseband will allow, and a froth of saliva covers his lips. "Our first trail ride this year," Dr. Cleveland explains. "I lunged him for a while, but he's still a bit fresh." She grins at me; there's a space between her front teeth that I've never noticed before. This must mean that despite having spent several hours in her company, including a couple of therapy sessions for when my mom was worried that I was bisexual, I've never seen her actually smile before, never seen her as happy as she is heading out on a trail ride on her barely-controlled 17.2 hand monster horse.

Now maybe I'm not the best one to judge, seeing as how

I can become terrified of things that might well be totally imaginary, but it seems to me that there are some things in life that people should be scared of, objective obvious things like huge horses with steam pouring out their nostrils.

"He'll be fine," says Kansas, heading to the out-gate. I guess she's saying this to me, because Dr. Cleveland doesn't appear to need any comforting. "I'll go first. Sylvia, you go in the middle."

I see Dr. Cleveland shorten her reins and Braveheart lifts his head even higher and hollows his back. The last thing I want is Braveheart breathing down my neck. I'd rather take my chances on being picked off at the end of the line by the were-ape.

"I think I'll go last," I tell Dr. Cleveland. "You can go in the middle."

Braveheart lunges ahead as though agreeing with my suggestion. He steps outside the arena and then spies my new pink bike leaning against the barn and spooks halfway across the parking lot. I know exactly how he feels.

Dr. Cleveland laughs. "Oh he's like this every year on his first ride out of the ring." She laughs again. I don't think it's that funny. I wonder if she's laughing because deep down she's scared—my mom says people do that sometimes. Otherwise I don't understand; I can't see how she could possibly enjoy this.

Kansas has gone ahead and hasn't noticed Braveheart's antics. She's started up the fence line the same direction I went yesterday. Dr. Cleveland follows and Brooklyn eagerly takes up the rear.

Brooklyn doesn't seem worried at all. He's acting like he's heading out on a picnic with his friends, while I feel more like we're walking headfirst into a live episode of *Up Close and Dangerous* on Animal Planet.

But if Brooklyn is calm…maybe I did imagine everything. Maybe there's something strange happening to my brain and I had a visual hallucination. A tumor perhaps. Dr. Cleveland would know.

I urge Brooklyn to step faster and pull in beside Braveheart. Brooklyn pins his ears when he's in line with Braveheart's head, and threatens to bite him. Braveheart barely notices. He has other things on his mind it seems, as he stares up the path, the whites showing around his eyes. I'm shocked at Brooklyn's behaviour—has he not even noticed that Braveheart is three-and-a-half hands taller? Can I not count on anyone to be sensible?

I take a deep breath then sigh. "Dr. Cleveland, I was wondering something—"

"Wait a minute," says Dr. Cleveland. She checks Braveheart firmly with her right rein and he flips his head in the air. "Okay, Sylvia, you were saying?"

"It's a brain question. I know you're not at work."

"I don't mind," says Dr. Cleveland. She shortens her reins another couple of inches, so the bend comes totally out of her elbows. If she continues to ride him like this, he'll blow for sure. Maybe I shouldn't be distracting her, except that this were-ape stuff is eating me up.

"What if you think you see something that doesn't exist?" I say.

"Like what?"

Braveheart breaks into a jiggy trot and Dr. Cleveland yells at him to walk. He takes a few walk steps and Dr. Cleveland tells him he's a good boy.

I'm wondering if doctor-patient confidentiality applies when out on horseback, and decide to chance it.

"Say, sort of like a werewolf, but not really." To cover myself, I add, "Say on a trail ride, hypothetically."

Braveheart grinds his teeth. Dr. Cleveland reaches

forward with one hand to stroke his neck in a soothing sort of way which Braveheart takes no notice of whatsoever.

"Hypothetically?" says Dr. Cleveland. "Well, if you think you've seen something that you can't have seen because it doesn't exist, then I guess you've deluded yourself. You saw something else. This can happen easily, especially if you don't have time for a good look. Lawyers say that their worst evidence in a court of law is an eyewitness. Perception is a constructive process. I could be more technical…"

"No, that's good," I say, relieved that she hasn't talked about hallucinations or teen-onset schizophrenia, or other tragedies of mental health that my mom mentions on a regular basis.

"Especially if you have a concern on your mind already," says Dr. Cleveland. "For example if you're frightened after seeing a werewolf in a movie, you can trick yourself into thinking you've seen one somewhere else."

"Oh yeah. Kind of like how Mom tricks herself into seeing that I have an eating disorder, or Dad sees that we're wasting money all over the place and are headed for bankruptcy."

"Oh," says Dr. Cleveland. She's silent for a moment, then says, "That's the trouble with ideas all right: they attract evidence."

This is almost making me feel better. "There's just one thing, Dr. Cleveland. I haven't seen a werewolf movie for a long time, and when I did see one I didn't think it was scary. I thought it was dumb. I really don't think it's been on my mind."

"Maybe not a werewolf literally then, perhaps there's some sort of defense mechanism at work: displacement, for example," says Dr. Cleveland. "Maybe the werewolf stands for something similar that you're anxious about, or afraid of, or angry with."

"Something big and hairy?"

"Mm hmm."

We've caught up with Kansas who is waiting for us on the trail and she catches the end of the conversation. "You two talking about men?" she asks.

Dr. Cleveland laughs and says no.

Of course I have to wonder. I've been finding my dad scary lately, and spent some time closer to Franco than I ever have in my life and always found him scary even from a distance. Maybe it is something to do with men. But if this was the case, why would I imagine a big hairy creature with hairy breasts? Just remembering the creature makes my heart rate soar, and that's when Brooklyn finally gives in to temptation, reaches up and nips Braveheart firmly on the neck. Braveheart takes off, bouncing and straining to get his head down for a buck but Dr. Cleveland has him in a strangle hold, shortening her reins until they're about five inches long. Braveheart can't buck, but he can't relax either.

"Kelly, sit up!" shouts Kansas. "Don't lean forward! Turn him!"

They're heading for the branch in the trail.

"Go left!" I scream, startling Kansas who shoots me a brief puzzled look, then urges Hambone into a trot and we both pursue Dr. Cleveland who, just as I so desperately hoped, manages to take the left branch of the trail, avoiding the river, avoiding things that might exist or might not, and taking her in a big circle back to the barn.

# chapter
## nine

I'm sitting on Brooklyn, bareback, and there's no bridle, so that's a pretty good giveaway that I'm dreaming. Oh good. I could use a dream, with all the stress there is in my life right now.

We're riding on a trail. I recognize it. It's the one that goes down to the river. Since this is a lucid dream where I have control, I change the trail. I make it into an imaginary one that's nice and wide, with sunlight coming through the branches overhead, and bunnies beside us in the grass, and flowers growing, and baby robins peeping, and I can smell the freshness of the air, and hear the gurgling of the...river. Ack. We're at the river. How did this happen?

I try to turn the river into the ocean. I try to put us at the beach with sand and pebbles and seaweed and tidal pools with barnacles but the scene only lasts a few seconds then pops like a bubble and we're back at the river again.

We're not alone.

There is the creature, standing at the far bank, watching us. Then she turns (definitely a she) and walks, upright and full of grace, into the woods.

Not a bear. Taller than any gorilla I've ever seen on

National Geographic channel, and with longer straighter legs. Definitely not a human either.

"Wait!" I say. I can't believe I've said this. Wait? Wait so we can catch up and you can eat me? Except it's a dream of course. I can't get eaten in my own dream. Or I don't think I can. Brooklyn plows into the water. The river is deep in the middle, so he has to swim. I'm wearing my nightshirt and nothing else. I look down and see the wet fabric sticking to me and all my flatness. But as I watch, bulges form on my chest under my shirt, something that isn't supposed to happen until I start estrogen treatment, though of course in my dreams anything is possible. My nightshirt pulls apart at the neckline and falls off and when I look down again I'm covered with hair. Covered. Not secondary sexual characteristic hair. Total hair. Even more than Franco. Ugh.

I wake myself by consciously turning my head back and forth on my pillow.

I am obviously really screwed up.

It's Sunday morning, usually my favourite day for riding, but the last thing I want to do today is head out to the barn in case Kansas wants to drag me on another trail ride.

I figure I have some time to work up an excuse for my parents because they usually like to sleep in on Sundays. It used to be that they wanted extra "snuggle time," and I'd hear them in their room giggling, but now all they do is sleep. I've been hoping it's because people need more sleep as they get older so it's nothing for me to worry about.

When I arrive in the kitchen, Dad is already there, sipping a coffee and texting on his BlackBerry, so I guess he doesn't want cuddles or extra sleep.

I'm feeling pretty tense from my dream, but don't want to talk about it so I make a fake show of relaxed stretching and yawning—unnecessarily, as it turns out. Dad glances up briefly from his BlackBerry and says good morning. I pour myself a bowl of granola and spoon on some peach yoghurt. Dad has had toast for breakfast—I see the burnt crumbs on his plate. Usually he and Mom like a full cooked breakfast on Sunday. In the good old days I made them French toast and served it to them in bed.

Dad pockets his BlackBerry, leans over and plops a hand on my head and ruffles my hair which fortunately I haven't combed yet. I hate it when he does this. I think about saying, "Woof," but then Dad says, "Going riding today, Munchkin?"

"No," I say, "Kansas wants Brooklyn to have a day off." That was easy.

Dad nods as though this is completely plausible, but just in case, I add, "And I have an essay to research for school."

"Sure," says Dad. I can't believe that he would buy this crock. His attention is obviously elsewhere. His BlackBerry chimes from his pocket and he checks the display. "Great!" he says, getting up from the table. "I have a lesson with the golf pro at nine."

A lesson? I thought my dad knew everything about golf. Why would he need a lesson? Is he lying to me? My dad? But then…well, I'm lying to him.

After Dad leaves, before I can even finish my granola, Mom wanders into the kitchen, yawning and stretching, exactly like I did for Dad.

We've turned into a pack of liars.

"Dad has a golf lesson," I tell her.

"Oh that's good," she says.

"Why does Dad want lessons?" I ask.

"He tells me he's been having trouble with his long game," says Mom. "He's not getting the same distance on his fairway shots as he used to. He thinks he's losing power. Of course he's not as young as he used to be. Men have trouble accepting that."

I sense a lecture brewing on gender differences, which I've heard way too much about in the last few years, so I change the subject. "I'm giving Brooklyn a day off," I say.

She nods. "Good idea."

Do my parents not know me at all? When have I ever not wanted to go to the barn? This is as out of character as it would be if Dad suggested we take his American Express card and go have a good time.

Mom pours herself a mug of coffee. "I think I'll take Auntie Sally out for lunch. Do you want a ride over to visit with Taylor?"

Just what I don't need—time with Taylor who will want to teach me how to be an animal communicator. "No thanks, Mom, I'll be fine here on my own." This will give me time to do what I really need to do: research, but not for a dumb school essay.

I have to wait for Mom to leave before I can sit down in private in front of the computer. I press my palms together, concentrating on my problem and how to frame it with the right key words for Google. There are so many choices: hallucinations, bears, exotic animals, brain tumors, anxiety, defense mechanisms. I groan aloud at the thought of my problem being psychological, which would sooner or later attract my mom's attention and ruin my life. So I decide to eliminate these possibilities from my search. I would rather I had seen a real were-ape than that I imagined it—for any reason.

I start by Googling *werewolf.*

The werewolf movie I saw months ago wasn't scary, but the pictures on the Internet are another matter. They show werewolves being so gruesome and bloodthirsty that I wonder how much I want to learn about them. But I feel mesmerized by the pictures, in the same way that I was mesmerized by the alien movie when I was young and couldn't stop watching until I was practically petrified with terror.

I force myself to take my eyes off the computer screen and think sensibly for a moment. After all, I don't really believe that what I saw was a werewolf. The creature I saw definitely didn't have a wolf face because there was no long pointy snout. On the other hand, werewolves could be similar to dogs, where there are a lot of variations in facial features. Kansas's dog Bernadette has a pointy nose because she's part German shepherd. Taylor's dog Bunga is part pug and his nose is flat, as though he ran face-first into a cement wall several times (which wouldn't surprise me, because he is so slow to learn). Bernadette and Bunga don't even look like they're the same species, so maybe the same applies to werewolves, in which case, I should scroll through all the pictures I can find.

After five minutes my pulse is racing and I'm wanting to lock all the doors in the house and nail the windows closed. Werewolves are totally menacing, with lots of long teeth and lean muscle. Not that I believe in them. Clearly they are imaginary—I do get that. Well, mostly I get that. But part of my brain is terrified.

I take several deep breaths and try to focus and steady my brain.

I decide to make a list of the differences between the creature I saw and a werewolf. I sift through the Wikipedia article for information, even though my teacher Mr. Brumby insists that this is not a reliable source of information and he won't accept it as a source for any essays we write for his class.

Werewolves are menacing and aggressive but the creature I saw disappeared as though she was frightened of me.

In pages and pages of information there was no indication that werewolves liked to fish.

Werewolves have long tails and perky ears. I can't remember my creature having either.

There are absolutely no werewolves with ape-like or pug faces.

Werewolves have long sinewy necks. The creature I saw had a neck shorter than Franco's.

As I study my list I realize that, unlike when I was young and frightened by the violence of that stupid alien movie, I'm not afraid that the creature I discovered will eat me or attack me, because she showed no sign of aggression. I haven't feared for my life these last few days; more I've feared for my sanity. It's the weirdness that has been deeply troubling. Not being able to understand what I saw has thrown me off-kilter.

I decide I need to do another search. This time I don't use Google, but go to Dogpile which is a metasearch engine that Mom is always telling me is better for finding scientific information. Mr. Brumby would be proud of me too. Not that I care.

I enter *were-ape* on the search bar.

There's some funny goofy stuff on YouTube, and not much else until I notice some interesting information about ape and human evolution in an article about *Ardipithecus ramidus*. To read more than the abstract I have to set up a free membership with an online science magazine, so I enter my mom's name and what I remember of her credentials as a registered therapist and her university degrees, and then I am granted access. The full article is pretty technical and frankly way over my head. But several of the diagrams are interesting. Even though the drawings are all of skeletons, I think if I added flesh and lots of hair, I would have something that looked like what I saw: an upright ape, long extinct.

Not a werewolf.

Not a were-ape.

My heart is racing again, but from excitement now, not fear. I have made an earth-shattering scientific discovery.

I print off the article and stash it in my backpack. I can hardly wait to discuss it with Logan Losino.

# chapter
## ten

Monday morning is going fine until I grab my backpack, stumble into the garage and stub my eyes on the pink and white abomination. I can't do it. I can't ride it to school. The teasing would be unbearable.

I also can't leave it in the garage. If my dad notices I'm not using something he paid perfectly good money for, he'll go ballistic. I know, because that's what happened when my mom didn't use the spa gift certificate for laser hair removal that he bought her for her birthday. He said it was non-refundable and if she didn't redeem it, then next year he won't buy her anything. Mom said that's fine with her.

The other reason I can't leave Pinky in the garage is that I have to be able to bike to the stable after school. So I have to stash it somewhere, not on our property, and I don't have much time to find a place.

I pedal through the neighborhood, well off my usual bike route that would take me in a loop out into the country past Kansas's farm. Instead I take much the same path I used when I had to walk to school. I cruise through suburbia, looking for a hiding place—a shed, a bush, something.

I'm going slowly so I don't miss any opportunities,

otherwise I never would have noticed Logan Losino as I round a corner, sitting on the front steps of a brown two-storey house, rubbing his hands together, searching the road in my direction.

He leaps to his feet when he sees me which makes me feel pretty happy but then he slows and strolls to the bottom of his driveway so casually that I have to doubt he's meaning to meet me at all. I feel confused, and am inclined to pedal on past him, except that Logan might know a good hiding place for Pinky. I decide to stop. I wait beside Pinky at the edge of the road. As Logan approaches I catch a whiff of that horse liniment smell. Could Franco be around? I peer around Logan but can't see Franco anywhere, and as Logan draws closer I realize that he is the source of the smell. Of course it's not horse liniment, I know that. Maybe it's some other medicated product, such as shampoo. The whole Losino family could have some sort of contagious hair condition, like dandruff. If Logan wasn't so much taller than me I could check.

Logan stands in front of me, bouncing on his toes. "You're riding this way to school now?" he says. He hasn't even noticed the hideous Pinky. He must be colour blind. I remember from one of my mom's gender difference lectures that this is much more common in boys than girls.

"My dad bought me a new bike," I say. I don't want Logan to feel self-conscious about his colour blindness, so I steer clear of mentioning the ghastly pinkishness. "Obviously it's meant for a six-year-old. Amber and Topaz..." My voice catches unexpectedly and I can't finish the sentence but Logan nods understandingly so I say, "I have to hide it somewhere. I'm not taking it to school."

Logan doesn't even take time to think, and he doesn't assess the bike at all, he just takes my word for it. It's as though he's been presented with some sort of once-in-a-life-time opportunity and doesn't have a second to waste. "Put it in our garage," he says urgently. "You can hide it there every day. I'll show you the side door."

Logan grabs my bike, vaults onto the seat and pedals up the driveway. The bike is so small for him that his knees come up around his elbows and he has to hunch over the handlebar. He looks like a cute circus bear.

He's almost at the top of the driveway up by the house when Franco comes out the front door. Franco has his gym bag in one hand and a math textbook in the other. He must be doing remedial math because it's the same one I'm using. Franco takes one look at Logan and goes crazy. "You stupid fairy! What do you think you're doing? If I ever see you at school on a pink bike you're dead!" He flings the book and it hits the front wheel and breaks in two down the binding. Loose pages flutter across the driveway. I can't say I've never wanted to do that to a math book, but still I find Franco pretty scary.

"It's not my bike, you moron," says Logan. "It's Sylvia's. I'm hiding it in the garage for her." He reaches to open the side door of the garage, but Franco stops him.

"She's not going in there," says Franco.

Logan looks at Franco and shakes his head. "Oh here we go again. Fine. I'll put the bike in the shed." Logan goes out of his way to drive over a page, then disappears around the back of the house, calling for me to follow.

I give Franco a wide berth and manage to time it so he's bending to pick up some pages when I slip past.

I find Logan around the corner tucking Pinky in beside another bike in a garden shed. I take off my helmet and loop the chinstrap over my bike's handlebar. Pinky looks even more ridiculous in comparison with the other bike, which is black and red, has no sparkles, and the frame is so thick it looks like it could carry an elephant.

"This is my mountain bike," says Logan. "It's full-suspension." He shows me the front shocks and the heavy-duty spring in the frame. "You wouldn't believe what I can do with this baby."

"You don't ride it to school?" I ask.

"No way," says Logan. "It's not a road bike. It's made for trails and jumping off cliffs. Besides, someone would steal it. I had to save for months to buy it." He checks his watch. "We better hurry if we want to get to school on time." He grabs my hand, and together we run back to the driveway— where Franco is waiting for us.

# chapter
## eleven

Franco has the pieces of the book in one hand and he shakes them at Logan. "Look what you made me do. I'm going to be in big trouble with Brumby over this, you little fag."

Logan's hand vibrates in mine.

"You did it yourself, dumbo," says Logan.

Franco looks from Logan to me and gives me a thorough once-over, from head to toes and back again. It's as though he's never really seen me before. Maybe he hasn't. Maybe he never noticed me whenever he was with Taylor.

"This is my girlfriend, Sylvia," says Logan.

My eyes almost pop right out of my head. His girlfriend? I am? Well, perhaps only to deflect Franco, who apparently believes that Logan is gay. I think of all the times that Logan has come to my rescue.

I clear my throat. "Yes," I say.

Franco looks me up and down again and scoffs. "Are you sure that's a girl?" he says. "How old is she—five?"

I feel Logan's grip tighten. He won't understand that I'm used to these sorts of comments. I don't want him to confront Franco on my behalf. I give his hand a tug. "Come on, Studly," I say, because that's what my mom used to call my dad in the good old days.

"Studly?" says Franco, laughing. He picks up his gym bag and swings it over his shoulder. "Now I've heard everything." Shaking his head, he swaggers away down the driveway.

Logan stoops and picks up a rock.

"No, Logan. He's not worth it."

Logan studies the rock in his hand.

"You'll only make him mad," I say.

"Not if I kill him first."

"You can't play pro ball if you have a criminal record," I remind him.

He turns to me and smiles. "You remember me saying that?"

I tell him of course I remember.

"I suppose there are smarter ways of taking revenge," he says, tossing the rock under a shrub.

We run together down the driveway, along the road, past lumbering Franco, and finally when I can't run any more I make him walk. He continues to hold my hand. When we reach the corner by Amber and Topaz's house I expect him to let go, but he doesn't. It's as though he's proud.

Even when we've stopped running, my palm keeps sweating. I like holding hands with Logan and at the same time I don't. I mean, what's next? Is he going to want to put his arm around me? Is he going to try to slide his hand up under my shirt? I sneak a look at his face, as though this might give me an idea about his intentions, but he's smiling at me in the friendliest sort of way, reminding me of all the years I've known him in school, and how he's always been nice to me, and always been a jokester, and really he's pretty cute even though he's having a little trouble with some acne at the back of his neck. But what the heck does he see in me?

Franco's right about that. I figure Logan could hold hands with any girl in school, and instead he picks the shrimp who still wears an undershirt instead of a bra. I don't understand. I hope he doesn't want to kiss me—I'm not ready for that. My mom has warned me about boys, how they are propelled by testosterone to only think about one thing, which I take to mean sexual intercourse, and I'm really not ready for that.

I wonder if there's such a thing as a pulley rein stop for boys like there is for runaway horses—not that Logan is running away with me. Something more subtle could work. Kansas says that sometimes horses just need a distraction from what they're thinking about. I remember the article I have about *Ardipithecus*.

"Logan, can I talk to you about something?" I say.

"Anything," he says.

"You have to promise not to laugh."

"I promise," says Logan and he crosses his heart with his free hand. Maybe kissing him wouldn't be so bad, though not right now.

I make myself focus. I take in a deep breath and let it out. I square my shoulders the way Kansas has taught me to, lift my sternum and feel the balance in my feet. "I saw something, when I was riding," I tell him. "I thought at first it was a bear, but it wasn't. I think I saw an extinct ape."

Logan doesn't laugh, thank goodness. He squeezes my hand. "Wow. Have you told anyone else?" he says.

I shake my head, then remember. "I had a hypothetical discussion with Dr. Cleveland." I'm not sure about telling Logan that Dr. Cleveland is my former therapist, and decide that saying anything about this now would only confuse the matter. "She's a psychiatrist who has a horse at my barn. I told her I thought I saw a were-ape, but that was before I found out about *Ardipithecus*—though I guess it could be either. Anyway, she thinks maybe I've deceived myself into believing I saw something because I'm afraid."

"Afraid of what? I didn't think you were afraid of anything…except maybe for Amber and Topaz." Logan is making a little joke, but I don't mind. It actually feels kind of nice that he knows me so well.

"I could be subconsciously afraid," I say. "Though that sounds like something my mom would think. She's a psychotherapist."

"Cool," says Logan, which almost makes me drop his hand.

"You have no idea," I say. "And my dad's a financial planner. They're both obsessed."

Logan shrugs. "All adults are obsessed about something," he says.

"Even your parents?"

"My mom's a teacher. There's nothing worse than having a teacher for a parent, unless it's having a parent who's a teacher at your own school. Fortunately I don't have that to deal with. As it is, I can't get away with anything. When she asks 'How was school today?' she really means it."

I imagine what it would be like if one of my parents was a teacher, and have to agree with Logan: nothing would be worse. At least I enjoy some peace for a few hours a day, and I can brush off questions about how school is going because they don't have a clue.

"What about your dad?" I say. "What's his obsession?"

Logan hesitates so long that I start to think I shouldn't have asked, that maybe his dad has a top secret profession such as a spy, or an undercover law enforcement officer.

Eventually he clears his throat and tells me his dad is a biologist, which doesn't sound strange at all, and I want to ask Logan what the problem is when he says, "My dad's always going on about global warming and climate change and how humans are a scourge on the face of the planet and Earth would be better off without us."

"That is harsh," I say.

"How do you know you saw an extinct ape?" asks Logan.

"I found an article on the computer with a drawing of a skeleton and a ton of text. I think it describes what I saw, though I don't understand all of it."

"Let me read it," says Logan.

I slip off my backpack and we're digging through the front pocket for the article when Amber shows up.

"Looking for her flea powder?" she says.

"Nope," says Logan. "Bear spray." He stands and faces her with one hand behind his back. He's holding the article rolled up in his fist, but of course Amber doesn't know that. She looks at the place where his arm disappears, then searches Logan's face, looking for a sign, perhaps of Logan's usual humour and good will.

Logan doesn't flinch.

"Oh I was just kidding," says Amber, backing away. She scampers around us, laughing in a forced way. "I'll see you at school!" she says over her shoulder.

"Not if I see you first," says Logan under his breath. He puts a smile on his face and he waves, so I wave too for a few seconds, then I stop. I don't like this fakeness. I don't like pretending to be friendly when I'm not. It worries me that this is how people have treated me all my life, pretending to accept me but believing I'm a weirdo misfit midget.

"Logan," I say, "we don't have to do this. Let's go." I take his hand. *I* take *his* hand. I can't believe it, but I do. It frightens and excites me, thinking what I might come up with next.

# chapter
## twelve

School is pretty boring, all day, though any time I bring my hand near my nose, I can smell Logan Losino, so that's kind of fun. Plus I tell myself I'll never get dandruff on my palm which is a good thing, and it makes me laugh inside even when Mr. Brumby continues his reign of terror by springing a surprise quiz on us in math class.

Logan is waiting for me at the front door after school. For a change there's no sign of Amber or Topaz, so I guess they have dance lessons. Logan walks me back to his place where Pinky is stashed. There's no sign of Franco either; he's probably at the gym learning how to bench-press small children.

I'm buckling on my helmet when Logan says, "Can I come with you?"

I freeze with my fingers stuck on my chinstrap. "It would be boring," I say.

"No, it wouldn't. Not as much as homework."

I can't see how I can get out of this. I wonder if I should tell him that Kansas has a No Boys policy at the barn, but that would make Kansas sound sexist and I don't want to do that.

"It's boring watching people ride," I tell him. "I stay in the arena during the week. I go around in circles. I'm not even jumping Brooklyn yet." Truly, I don't want him to come. I don't want to have to split my attention between Brooklyn and Logan. I don't know how to tell him this. He sees my hesitation, and looks down at his toes. I've hurt his feelings. He's been so nice to me, and I've been mean to him. I feel awful.

"How about another time?" I say.

His face lights up. "On a weekend? When you're not in the arena? We could explore the trails. My bike can go anywhere a horse goes."

"Sure," I say. "That's a great idea." Though it isn't of course. For one thing, bikes can't jump fallen trees. For another, I don't intend to do another trail ride for the rest of my life.

Declan's truck is parked beside Kansas's beater near the barn, but there's no sign of them until I open the tack room door, and there they are, necking, shirtless (both of them!), in a panic of motion when they hear the door squeak on its hinges.

I could die, I really could.

Kansas isn't even wearing a sports bra. She's got some frilly pink thing on, that hardly has her covered at all. Pink. I can't believe it.

Declan turns his back and pulls a black T-shirt over his head. He saunters past me without a word.

"Ooops—sorry," says Kansas.

"Couldn't you have gone to your trailer?" I ask. This would have been so simple. The trailer is mere steps away, behind the barn.

"We got a bit carried away," says Kansas, as though this is an explanation. "I didn't plan on it."

"If you weren't planning on it why weren't you wearing your sports bra?" I ask.

Kansas stops buttoning her shirt. "There's no need to be mad at me," she says.

"I'm not mad," I say. Then I think about it, and realize I am, a little bit, though I couldn't say why. It's not that I'm jealous of Kansas's attentions. It's more like I feel she's betrayed me. What's that about?

"This *is* my barn," says Kansas.

Sure it's her barn. She has every right, that's not the problem. Still, I'm feeling really upset with her, plus upset with myself because I can't figure out why. I'd like to punch something—hard.

Kansas finishes doing up her shirt except for one section where two buttons are missing, then she stands there looking at me sheepishly, as though she thinks she's done something wrong too. I can tell she feels guilty, which somehow makes me feel more upset, and so even though it's not very nice of me, I find myself taking advantage of the situation. "Can you give me a riding lesson?" I ask. "I'd like to do some jumping."

Kansas has been reluctant to help me start jumping with Brooklyn. She wants us to perfect our flat work first, something that could take the rest of my life at the rate we're going. I know Kansas loves dressage, I know that flat work is important, but I want to jump.

Kansas is ready to roll out her usual objections. She shakes her head and I see her mouth open to say no.

I say, "My parents think it's okay. They trust you. They think you're very wholesome and provide a safe learning environment."

Kansas looks at the floor for a moment and then sighs. "Okay," she says.

"Not just ground poles," I tell her. "I want to really jump something."

"Fine," she says.

When I've tacked up Brooklyn and led him to the ring, Kansas is out there, pacing out the distances between the jumps.

We do our usual flat work for ten minutes to warm up. Brooklyn is a slug. It's all I can do to get him moving forward. He is so bored with this. Like me.

Finally Kansas tells me to shorten my stirrups two holes and we review how to balance in a forward seat with weight in my heels. Kansas tells me I'm a natural. She says it like she's not entirely happy about it, like it would be better if I was a slower learner and needed to spend more time on the flat. I'm thrilled anyway, and when she tells me to, I ride Brooklyn through a grid of ground poles with a one-foot jump at the far end. Actually, it's not big enough to be called a jump. Even Kansas only calls it a bounce, but it's a start.

Brooklyn clears it by a mile, then brings his head way up, tosses it and pulls into the bridle, much like he did on the trail ride.

Kansas tells me to circle him until he slows down. After about the twentieth circle she says to stop him and wait while she finds a running martingale in the tack room. I hope Declan hasn't crept back there or I'll be waiting forever. His truck is still in the parking lot. I don't know where he's gone.

But Kansas returns quickly with the martingale, and I dismount and she shows me how to slip it over Brooklyn's neck, run the girth through the long end, and pass the reins through the metal rings.

"He likes to jump," says Kansas.

"A lot," I say.

"The martingale will give you some leverage. I don't like gizmos on horses, but he has a strong neck. I don't want him running off with you."

I snort. "I can control him. He listens really well to emergency stop aids."

Kansas slows as she refastens the rein buckle, so I realize what I've done. She slips the end through its keeper. "And when exactly did you do an emergency stop on Brooklyn?" she asks.

I lead Brooklyn to the mounting block, wondering how much I can say, or better still, how little I can say.

I step onto the mounting block and Brooklyn positions himself beside me. He's still excited, his neck is up and he's looking at the closest jump in the ring. I stick my toe in the stirrup and swing into the saddle.

"It was last week sometime," I say, hoping she'll be satisfied with a vague answer. No such luck.

"And what exactly were the circumstances?" says Kansas.

I can't brush her off. If I try, she'll stop my jumping lesson.

"He took me on a trail ride," I say.

"*He* took *you*?" says Kansas.

"I put him on a loose rein, and let him go where he wanted." Kansas doesn't say anything, so I continue. "We went to the river."

"To the river?" says Kansas. Her voice is getting high. "Did you cross it?"

"Of course not," I say. "There was a..." Now what am I going to say? I don't want to explain the extinct ape thing to Kansas. Kansas doesn't use the Internet so she won't understand. "There was a bear," I tell her, "in the water. Fishing."

"Jesus," says Kansas.

"It was fine," I tell her. "Brooklyn was good. He got kind of excited, but then he...galloped me to safety."

"Oh lord," says Kansas.

"And I did a pulley rein stop before we had to turn that sharp corner where the trail divides. I did it exactly the way you taught me," I say. I pick up my reins and ask Brooklyn to trot down the long side of the ring, and we circle at the far end, giving Kansas some time to absorb all the news and come to the reasonable conclusion that no action needs to be taken given that no one was hurt and that Brooklyn took care of me and never got frightened. I was the one who was frightened, but I'm not going to tell her that.

We trot down the other long side. Kansas is in the middle of the ring considering her rubber boots. "What did your parents say about all this?" she asks.

I know what she's getting at. She wants to know how much trouble she's in for letting me go on a trail ride all by myself.

"I haven't told them yet," I say.

I figure this is a good way of influencing her to raise the jumps above baby height.

I trot through the grid, and Brooklyn sails over the bounce as usual, but I have better control on the far side thanks to the martingale. We do two circles, and I yell at Kansas, "Raise the last rail!"

She does. She puts it at two feet. Brooklyn jumps it as though it's twice that high, then we gallop off around the ring.

I'm so happy I could scream.

# chapter
## thirteen

The lesson is over and I'm riding Brooklyn on a loose rein until he cools off. I have to be careful not to let him stray too close to any of the jumps or he lurches towards them, hoping for another opportunity to play rocket-launcher. Kansas is moving a few of the jumps so they won't be in the way when Dr. Cleveland comes out for her ride this evening. I'm thinking how much I have enjoyed being an extortionist when Declan appears near the out-gate. Bernadette is cowering at his feet. This dog never cowers. When she sees Kansas, she bolts for her even though she's never allowed in the riding ring and is usually really good about staying outside.

Kansas must be too surprised to reprimand her. Bernadette shoves her nose between Kansas's knees and hides her head. Her tail is clenched tight and she's quivering all over.

Kansas strokes her, and looks to Declan. "What happened?" she says.

Declan shakes his head. "I have no idea. We went for a walk, and I thought I'd take the pup to the river to teach her to swim. She ran off down the trail ahead of me, then came tearing back as though her life depended on it. There was no way I could get her to the river after that, all she wanted to do was hide, or come home."

My eyelids have flown so wide apart I'm afraid my eyeballs may fall out. Fortunately Kansas isn't paying any attention to me (as usual when Declan is around). I clutch one trembling hand in Brooklyn's mane to steady myself.

"She must have seen a bear, maybe the same one Sylvia saw," says Kansas. "Or a cougar. Poor puppy."

"There are cougars around here?" says Declan looking back over his shoulder in the direction of the trail. I follow his gaze, aware that I would be relieved beyond words to see Declan's worst fear appear over the rise.

Kansas misses all this. She strokes Bernadette's back and coos, "You're safe now, Bernie, whatever you saw, silly puppy."

I'm thinking about what Dr. Cleveland said, and wondering if dogs could possibly be as capable of self-deception as humans are, and whether they have defense mechanisms like displacement, but somehow I don't think so. Dogs are more straightforward than that.

Kansas picks up Bernadette who has in my opinion grown too big for this sort of treatment, and carries her across the ring. When Kansas passes through the out-gate, Declan puts his arm around her shoulders, and together the three of them bumble off to the trailer behind the barn.

Neither of them noticed my bug eyes, my shaking hands. Only Brooklyn has sensed my anxiety and now, as though taking care of me, has settled into a slow plod. When he's cool, I dismount and lead him to the alleyway in the barn where he stands like a rock while I untack him. He doesn't even flinch when I pull the saddle off his back and forget about the martingale being connected to the girth and end up with a mess of saddle and straps around his feet.

I sort this out eventually, then brush him until all the sweat is removed from his coat, and I pick out his feet again, and brush his tail until there's not a single knot, and I realize I'm procrastinating. I'm still scared, and it's dusk, and I don't want to be riding my bike home alone. I'm turning into a weenie. I throw my arms around Brooklyn's neck, and hold him, thinking: I didn't imagine anything. I know what Bernadette saw. It's the same thing as I saw, and Brooklyn saw: the prehistoric ape, or a were-ape, truly it could be either.

Declan clears his throat behind me. I spring away from Brooklyn and try to look composed and self-assured.

"I thought I should give you a lift home," says Declan, "seeing as how there may be a cougar in the neighborhood."

"Sure," I say, though I think it's odd. I would have thought that Kansas would drive me if they were having concerns. I put Brooklyn in his stall, grab my backpack from the tack room, then meet Declan at his truck. The engine is running and I climb into the passenger seat, and that's when I remember Pinky. "My bike!" I say, knowing that the bed of Declan's truck is full of horseshoeing supplies, and his gas forge, and there won't be room for a bike back there. But Declan is out of the truck already, and I watch as he wheels Pinky from beside the barn, opens the crew cab door, picks up the bike like it's a feather and slides it in behind the front seats.

"New bike?" says Declan, taking his seat behind the steering wheel.

I sigh. "Yes. I hate it." I feel badly because I sound ungrateful, but Declan doesn't say anything. He's not the lecturing type. He's barely the speaking type most of the time. "It's pink," I explain, and I see him nod as I point left and we pull out onto the roadway. I tell him I live on Willow Crescent and he says he knows the way.

"You could paint the bike," he says. "What colour would you like it to be?"

"You're sure?"

He nods again. Declan knows all about metal of course, being a farrier.

"Silver would be good," I say.

Declan utters some vague sounds to the effect that he thinks this is possible. He makes a little coughing noise and clears his throat. "What you saw..." he says, then stops to gather his thoughts, and my heart pounds because I'm thinking he wants to talk about the were-ape, but then he says, "What you saw in the tack room—I need to apologize for that. I don't want you blaming Kansas. She's feeling guilty that she's let you down, and she's unhappy that you're angry with her."

Declan stops talking, which gives me time to gather my thoughts too. I stare off down the road ahead of us. Yes, I am mad at Kansas. I rerun the event in my mind. I picture opening the tack room door, and all I see is the pink bra. That's what's bothering me. Well, not the bra exactly. I'm upset because Kansas has always acted as though all that girly stuff was not important, and we could be kindred spirits in a gender-free sort of way, then Declan came along and, without my noticing, everything changed.

There's no way I can explain all of this to Declan. I can barely explain it to myself.

"Kansas could have talked to me herself," I say.

Declan nods. "You're right. But she's all emotional these days."

This makes me even more mad. I haven't been able to notice that Kansas is *all emotional* because I'm not getting any time with her.

I point out my house and Declan pulls into our driveway.

Neither of us says anything. We get out of the truck and Declan hauls Pinky from the cab. Declan is a good person. He apologized to me and I can't remember the last time an adult did that. I look up at him as he gives me my bike. "Declan, I accept your apology," I say, because that's what Mom says when I apologize to her, though she usually follows up with a lecture about where I went wrong in the first place.

The corner of Declan's mouth twitches. I guess he doesn't know what to say. He holds out his hand so we can shake on it.

I wish I was better at making conversation with people. I wish I had talked to Declan about the were-ape, but it's too late now. I settle for shaking his hand (which is mind-bogglingly strong and calloused). Maybe some things don't need to be said.

# chapter
## fourteen

I roll my bike into the garage, thinking it's been a long hard day, and then I notice my mom watching from the doorway and realize it's not over yet. She's all excited: her cheeks are rosy and she's bouncing from one foot to the other. Either she's won the lottery or she's been drinking way too much coffee.

"Aren't you having an interesting day!" she says, making bug-eyes at Declan as he backs out the driveway. She flutters a palm below her throat and bats her eyelashes. "Boys all over the place!"

Oh no. What else has happened? I'm not sure I have the energy to cope with any more emotional events today. Maybe if I don't say anything she'll leave me alone. I tuck Pinky in the corner then try to edge past Mom into the house. She pins me against the doorjamb.

"Sugarplum, you had a phone call!" She pauses for drama, as though we were in short supply. "From a B—O—Y!" she spells. We all know I have trouble with spelling, but this is ridiculous.

I close my eyes for a moment. A boy? There is a remote chance I would be excited if only Mom wasn't excited enough for both of us, basically ruining everything.

"Mom—"

"Didn't I tell you there'd be boys some day?" says Mom, proudly, as if she was responsible for this miraculous event.

As if I cared about boys.

As if I've ever cared about anything other than horses.

She hands me the cordless phone which she's been hiding behind her back. "I left a message in your room, but his number shows in the call display too."

I take the phone, but won't look at the display, not in front of Mom. I'll find out who called when I'm in my bedroom, where there won't be an audience. "Thanks, Mom."

"You're welcome, Honey. Let me know if you need to talk. It's a whole new world for you." She gives my shoulders a squeeze as I slide by.

The message in my room says to call Logan Losino ASAP.

Franco answers. At least I think it's Franco—he's the only one I could imagine grunting that way on the phone. I ask to speak to Logan. I hear Franco yelling for Logan to get his little fairy butt to the phone because his girlfriend is on the line. I can hear the sneer in his voice when he says *girlfriend.* It makes me want to hang up, but before I can, Logan says, "Hi Sylvia." So he knew it was me, which means I must be his only girlfriend, and that makes me feel better though I don't know why because I'm not sure I even want to be his girlfriend, or anybody's girlfriend.

"I read that article," says Logan. He's so excited that I can't get a word in edgewise. "And I couldn't understand all the terminology, and I didn't want to ask my dad because he can go off on some weird tangents but I was stuck so in the end I asked him, as casually as I could, and he explained some of it, but then he wanted to know why I was suddenly interested in *Ardipithecus,* so I told him I had a friend who'd seen one and that's when he went bananas."

"Oh no," I say. I should never have involved Logan. Now his dad thinks I'm a moron for believing I've seen an extinct prehistoric ape. He probably won't let me hide Pinky in his shed, and I'll have to bike all the way to school and be even more humiliated.

"Actually, it was great to see him so enthusiastic," says Logan. "We talked and talked. I haven't had so much fun with him in ages. He wants me to ask if you've told anyone else," says Logan.

"Only Dr. Cleveland, but she thinks—"

"Oh I told him about that, and he laughed and said her response was typical. Anyone else?"

"No one." I decide not to mention that I almost told Declan in case that made Logan jealous.

"Good," says Logan. "He doesn't think you should tell anyone, except your parents, because you need to ask their permission to talk to him. He wants to meet with you. He wants to know everything you saw."

"He wants me to tell my parents? Are you kidding? I'll never be allowed to ride again, my dad will lead a SWAT team into the woods…"

"My dad thinks you're amazing," says Logan. "He's really impressed with your research. He says *Ardipithecus* is interesting, but usually they think more along the lines of *Gigantopithecus*."

"What?" Now I'm really confused.

"He's been obsessed with these things for years. I couldn't tell you before because I never believed him, but I do now, because you saw one," says Logan.

I am so lost the best GPS in the universe wouldn't help me. "I saw one what?" I say.

"You saw a sasquatch," says Logan.

Over dinner I try and try to think of how to tell my parents. Mom is doing her best not to pry, but I can tell she's desperate to know about my phone call to the B—O—Y. She keeps glancing at me and blinking and raising her eyebrows meaningfully. Dad doesn't notice a thing. He doesn't even seem to be present. He twirls strands of spaghetti onto his fork, then lets them slide back into the sauce. He sighs heavily. "Sorry, I don't seem to have much appetite," he says.

Of course this draws Mom's attention away from me. Dad's at risk of breaking one of the family rules about cleaning one's plate because of the starving children in Darfur and because of the example one sets and because we certainly don't want Sylvia to develop an eating disorder. She doesn't say any of this—she doesn't have to—we've heard it all before. All she says, with her reminding tone is, "Ahem—Tony?"

"What?" says Dad.

Mom flicks her eyes in my direction.

"This is good, Mom," I say, digging in.

"I'm not hungry," says Dad.

"I'm working on a group science project at school," I say.

Mom says, "Tony, have you thought about seeing Dr. Destrie for a check-up?"

Dad drops his fork on his plate. A glob of sauce splashes onto his placemat. "That washed-up old fossil?" says Dad. "I'd rather go to a walk-in clinic."

"Tony," says Mom, this time with her warning tone.

"Not that I'm going to any clinic," says Dad. "There's nothing wrong with me."

I think about mentioning his short fuse, his bike-tossing, his car-hijacking, his elder abuse, but decide against it.

"I'm just a bit tired these days," says Dad.

"And no appetite," says Mom. "Of any variety," she adds.

At first I don't know what she's getting at, but then I figure it out. Oh god. This I didn't want to know.

"We have some homework and I need to go to Logan's house tonight after dinner," I say.

They both stare at me, Mom with a pleased smile, Dad with something else.

"Is *Logan* another of these New Age androgynous names that you girls have assimilated now?" says Dad.

"He wants to know if Logan is a girl," says Mom.

"She knows what I meant, I don't need you interpreting me to my own daughter," says Dad. A bottle of pills rattles as he drags it out of his pocket and he plunks it on the table in front of Mom. "I'm taking these. Jerry recommended them."

Mom examines the bottle. "You're taking a nutraceutical product called *Bali Mojo*? Do you even know what's in it?"

"It worked for Jerry."

"Do you have anything other than anecdotal evidence? Any scientific controlled studies?"

Oh boy. This is going to be a bad one. I finish the last of my spaghetti, and push my chair back from the table. "May I be excused?" I say. "I don't have room for dessert anyway. That was excellent, Mom." I rub my stomach appreciatively, and make it bulge as though it's really full. "I'll ride my bike to Logan's."

"I think not," Mom tells me, then turns back to Dad. "Logan is a boy. He lives on Alder Street. His dad is a government wildlife biologist and his mom is a teacher over at Southview Elementary. He has an older brother named Franco who has had some brushes with the law but I was unable to access the necessary records, so I'll be advising Sylvie to take some caution around him in the interim."

I stare at my mom. I can't believe it. I feel like my own privacy has been invaded. I also can't believe she hasn't made the connection with the Franco her niece is dating, unless this is something she and Auntie Sally never talk about, which would be strange. "You Googled them," I say.

Mom shrugs. "I used the reverse phone directory and did some online research, which is exactly what any responsible parent would do."

"What?" say Dad and I together.

Mom pats her lips with her napkin, then pushes back her chair. "I'll give you a lift, Honey, it's too dark to be riding your bike."

I manage not to talk to her all the way over. She knows exactly where she's going anyway because she's entered their address in the car's GPS. She tells me she'll pick me up in an hour. I try to slam the car door, but don't have the muscle for it of course, which only makes me more angry.

# chapter
## fifteen

Mom waits in the car while I ring the doorbell. I'm hoping that Franco will answer the door to give her a good scare, but Logan swings it open. Mom beeps the horn twice then drives away.

Logan stops me in the entranceway and studies my face. "What's the matter?" he says.

"My parents," I say.

"You told them?"

"Are you kidding? It was enough of an event to say I wanted to go to a boy's house after dinner. Anything more and the universe would have imploded."

Logan seems uncertain.

"I'll tell them later," I say, "after I've talked to your dad."

Logan leads me down a long hall and only then do I start worrying about what it's going to be like to meet his family and what they're going to think of me. I probably should have changed, but everything at home was running late, so I'm still wearing my riding pants with the suede patches on the inside of the knees. The pants taper at my ankles and fit inside my Ariat Junior Performer paddock boots, which of course have their patented self-cleaning treads so at least I don't have to worry about tracking horse manure through the Losinos' house. Plus I have serious hat hair from wearing my riding helmet. I run my fingers through it, trying to fluff it up and create some volume. Logan catches me. "You look fine," he says.

"I do?" I snort, then I say, "I don't think I ever look fine."

"You look like you," says Logan, as though this might actually be a good thing.

So then I start worrying about what his parents will be like. Maybe Logan is the family freak and everyone else is like Franco, which would make Mr. Losino's interest in sasquatches more understandable: it may be more like genealogy research to him, given Franco's resemblance to whatever it was I saw in the river.

Logan pushes a swinging door into the kitchen. He introduces me to his parents who look remarkably normal, but since my parents look pretty normal too, I know how insignificant this is. His dad is dishing up ice cream and his mom has been reading the paper. No sign of Franco, fortunately.

Mr. Losino tells me to take a seat at the table and he serves me a bowl of maple walnut ice cream which is not my favourite but of course I know better than to say so. I take a spoonful and tell him that it is delicious. Mrs. Losino is watching me carefully. I know what this is about. I have to say something or she'll be thinking her son is a pedophile.

"I have Turner Syndrome," I tell her. "I know I look like an eight-year-old, but really, I'm almost fifteen."

"Oh," says Mrs. Losino. She places a hand on my arm. "Thank you for telling me, Sylvia, though that isn't what I was thinking. I'm sorry if I was staring. It's just that I've been hearing about you since you were in grade one with Logan…"

"Mom!" says Logan.

She's been hearing about me? Like what a midget nitwit I am?

"Good things, of course," says Mrs. Losino.

"Mom!" says Logan.

Good things? Since grade one? Even I couldn't think of good stories about me from grade one.

Mrs. Losino sighs. "And then, on meeting you, I thought maybe you were another late bloomer, like Logan, which would be nice for him."

Logan makes a moaning sound and drops his forehead to the table.

Logan is a late bloomer? I always thought he was kind of perfect, in a boyish sort of way. But obviously she doesn't understand about Turner Syndrome. "I took human growth hormone for a while, but it increased my intracranial pressure and I had to stop, so I will always be short. I'm supposed to start estrogen therapy soon. Who knows what side effects I'll have to that. I may never bloom."

After a moment, Mrs. Losino nods her head. "I'm sorry, I think my choice of the phrase *late bloomer* was unfortunate," she says.

"I'll second that," says Mr. Losino. "She looks pretty blooming good to me just the way she is."

Now I see where Logan gets his sense of humor.

Not that he's finding any of this very funny apparently. He's still hiding his face. Mr. Losino punches him on the shoulder. "Get it, Logan? *Blooming good?*"

Logan lifts his head, looks at me and rolls his eyes. "I get it, Dad," he says.

Mrs. Losino tells us she has some lessons to prepare and she'll leave us to it.

I'm left in the kitchen with Logan and his dad.

As soon as Mrs. Losino disappears, Mr. Losino adds

three extra scoops of ice cream to his bowl then reaches into the back of the refrigerator and brings out a wide-mouthed white plastic container which he carries back to the table. There's a blue and white label identifying it as "Copper Sulfate Crystals" and there's a skull and crossbones over some text that's too small for me to read. "Want some?" he says to Logan.

I have to admit, I don't have much experience with the dinner table rules of normal families (my own and Auntie Sally's don't qualify), so I have to make an effort to be open-minded, but having poison crystals sprinkled on my dessert is way more than I can handle.

Mr. Losino unscrews the cap, turns the container upside down, and a bottle of Hershey's chocolate syrup lands in his palm. Now why would that have to be stored in a container? We never have it at our house. I've asked Mom to buy it for us, but she says it's full of sugar and palm oil and saturated fat and having it in the kitchen would be like pointing a loaded gun at my father's aorta.

Mr. Losino squirts about a cup of the stuff over his ice cream, then offers it to me and Logan. Logan says no way, but I'm still mad at my mom, plus I think the chocolate will be perfect for camouflaging the maple walnut flavour, so I hold out my bowl and get a big puddle of it. I hope Mom won't be able to smell it on my breath. Mr. Losino puts the ice cream back in the freezer compartment, then re-packages the syrup and tucks it in behind some other storage containers in the fridge.

"I told you your mom wouldn't find it in there, Logan," says Mr. Losino.

"Franco either," says Logan.

They hide chocolate syrup. Perhaps this isn't a normal family either.

"Logan tells me you saw something interesting down at the river," says Mr. Losino, taking his seat at the table. He stirs his ice cream into total mush, something I'm never allowed to do. At my house this would be referred to as "playing with your food," punishable by death-by-lecture.

I drag my attention away from Mr. Losino's bowl. I nod. I'm not sure what to say.

"You want to tell me about it?" says Mr. Losino. A dribble of mush is caught in his beard. I try not to stare, not that it would matter, because Mr. Losino isn't looking at me at all.

"Okay," I say, and then my brain seizes up and I can't think of what words to use. Mr. Losino doesn't prompt me, which helps me relax. He slurps his ice cream as though we've got all the time in the world. Logan smiles encouragingly.

"At first I thought it was a bear," I say.

Mr. Losino grunts and says, "That's what most people think when they see one."

"Then I saw it move, and it was so powerful and graceful that it reminded me of a werewolf I saw in a movie, except it didn't have a face like a wolf, so I thought it might be a were-ape."

Mr. Losino nods his head. "Interesting hypothesis."

He's not telling me I'm stupid, or mentally ill, or that I'm deceiving myself. This is great. So I tell him about talking to Dr. Cleveland and how she said that ideas attract evidence and perhaps I'd already been thinking about large scary things, at which point Logan interrupts and says, "Such as Franco, for example."

They laugh, and eventually I join in to show that I'm not scared of Franco either. At least not at the moment.

I explain about my Google research and how I found the article on *Ardipithecus* which was interesting because it was about an upright ape, not a knuckle-walker, though most of the article was beyond me so I gave it to Logan to help translate.

Mr. Losino says, "That was some impressive research you did. You could think about pursuing a career in science."

A scientist! I haven't thought of that. All I've ever wanted to be is the best rider possible. Maybe if I worked part-time as a scientist I would earn enough money and have time to ride. I like doing research on the Internet so this could be perfect for me…but then I remember. "I'm really bad at math," I say.

Mr. Losino shrugs as though this is not significant. "You have an active enquiring mind, which is more important in my opinion. You persist with your research until you find answers that make sense to you. Really, your finding the similarity to *Aridipithecus ramidus* is quite remarkable, though I've been focusing on *Gigantopithecus* myself."

Logan mutters something about Francopithecus that I don't quite catch.

"Though we have to admit that both *Ardipithecus* and *Gigantopithecus* have been extinct for quite a while so what you saw down by the river is clearly something else," says Mr. Losino. Finally he looks me in the eye. "You're a very lucky person. I've been wanting to see one my whole life. All I've ever found is footprints." He pushes his chair back from the table. "Come on, I'll show you the plaster casts." He swings open a door to a dark stairwell at the back of the kitchen. He flicks on a light which doesn't make a lot of difference, and I really wonder what I'm getting myself into this time but I follow him and Logan down into the basement, where I learn everything I never knew about sasquatches.

# chapter
## sixteen

Every morning for the rest of the week I ride Pinky to meet Logan, and he takes my hand and walks with me to school, and just before he leaves me at my locker he says, "Have you told them yet?" and I have to say no.

Mr. Losino has asked me to tell my parents as soon as possible, because he wants me to take him to where I saw the sasquatch so that he can add to his research project, and he won't do that without my parents' permission.

I can't tell them. I know how they would react. My mom would go all psychoanalytic on me, which would be even worse than what Dr. Cleveland had to say, and Dad would be overprotective and take out a big game hunting license and buy a gun.

So I put it off. I didn't even say anything to Mom when she picked me up at the Losinos' that first night and I was busting with all sorts of information about sasquatches. Mom wasn't very talkative anyway, so I figured she and Dad had a major dust-up while I was out of the house.

Mr. Losino has recommended I not tell anyone else, and that after I do tell my parents, I'm not to let them call anyone, such as the newspaper, or the police, Fish and Game, Wildlife Services, or National Defense. Mr. Losino said that no one would believe us or they'd make it into a big circus. He said definitely not to call a circus either. Not even Cirque de Soleil, which I understand has a better reputation than most.

There's one more reason I'm not telling my parents. I don't want to go back to the river, even accompanied by a sasquatch scientist. As long as I don't tell Mom and Dad, Mr. Losino won't be able to take me on that investigative field trip.

Every day I can see how disappointed Logan is, even though he tries to hide it.

Every night I dream I'm at the river and see the sasquatch, and I try to take charge of the dream and make the sasquatch disappear, but I can't do it. Plus I always end up being covered with hair in places I'm not supposed to have it even after I develop secondary sexual characteristics. The worst part is that I've become so paranoid that in the mornings I examine myself carefully and I swear I'm starting to see hair growing on my chest. I have to hold the flashlight really close to my skin, at an awkward angle, not shining in my eyes, and it's like I'm covered with this downy baby fur and I'm sure it wasn't there before.

I know I have an active imagination, and once in the past I convinced myself that I was a hermaphrodite and another time I thought I was some sort of human/unicorn hybrid, but there was no real evidence for any of that... except for the bony lump on my forehead which I still have. Still, the hair is not imaginary. It's really there, and I have no idea why.

I can't tell anyone either. They would want to see.

Granted, I have told Brooklyn because I can tell him anything and everything and he just accepts it—not that being covered by hair would be a problem from his point of view. I don't know what I would do without Brooklyn, even though he's not very impressed with me these days because I won't ride him outside of the ring, and unless Kansas is there I'm not allowed to jump, and Kansas always says she's too tired or she's not feeling well. I don't know what's gotten into her. She never used to be like this.

I guess I could talk to Taylor, but whenever I see her in the cafeteria she's with that big lump Franco and I'm afraid she'll tell him, and then he would tell Logan, and my life would be ruined.

So I have two secrets weighing on me, and at the end of the week I'm done.

On Friday night during dinner, I decide I have to tell my parents about the sasquatch. I do some deep breathing exercises. I square my shoulders. I don't have to wait for a pause in the conversation because no one's saying anything. I clear my throat. That's when the phone rings. It's Grandpa calling from Saskatchewan. Mom takes the call when she hears his voice on the answering machine even though we're not supposed to talk to anyone during family meal times. She takes the cordless phone out of earshot into the family room. Dad pulls out his BlackBerry and reads his text messages and laughs. I sit by myself and play with my mashed potatoes, wishing I had some chocolate syrup.

The evening deteriorates badly from this point.

Mom comes back to the table and reports that Grandpa has found a great last minute seat sale with WestJet. He'll be here tomorrow and he's staying two weeks.

"Tomorrow?" says Dad. "For two weeks? What are we supposed to do with him for two whole weeks?"

"He wants to see how Sylvia is doing with Brooklyn," says Mom.

"He could do that in one day," says Dad.

"What do you care, you're going to be working all the time anyway," says Mom. "Or playing golf."

"I will not," says Dad. "I'm a better host than that."

I used to not worry too much when my parents argued because they always made up, but that doesn't seem to happen any more. Mom used to get uptight and quote textbooks and Dad would make jokes until she started to laugh, then they would go to their bedroom. Now Mom stays pretty calm and Dad goes volcanic, and no one makes any jokes. I used to be pretty disgusted at their making-up sessions, but now I wish those days were back.

Mom isn't giving any ground, not that she was ever any good at that. I notice she has her non-face on, the expressionless mask she learned to use for her psychotherapy work. Something's up. I hope Grandpa isn't sick. I hope he isn't making one last trip out to see us before he dies.

"Besides," Mom says, "we probably won't have to entertain him at all this time. He's bringing a friend." Her professional face is crumbling. Is she trying not to cry? She slices a miniscule cube off her pork chop and stabs it with her fork but leaves it on the plate.

Dad doesn't notice. He's trying to load a pile of meat, potatoes and peas onto his fork and the peas keep falling off. "Great," he mutters. "Two senile old farts to watch over."

"Dad!" I say.

"Not exactly," says Mom. "He's bringing his girlfriend."

# chapter
## seventeen

We don't even have to pick them up at the airport. Grandpa says there are so many things Isobel wants to see that it will be better if they rent a car.

Our Saturday is shot anyway, because we have to tidy the house and make up the guest room and Mom tries to sound breezy and carefree when she says that Grandpa told her one bed would be fine, but it's bothering her. It kind of bothers me too, if I let myself think about it.

Plus we have to go grocery shopping, meaning me and Mom. She insisted Dad not cancel his golf game, she said she didn't want that noble selfless sacrifice hanging over her head, whatever that means. Dad squealed his tires on the way out the driveway, so he wasn't very happy about it. Maybe he didn't want to play golf today?

Mom and I drop in on Auntie Sally on the way home from Safeway. Mom says she needs to give Auntie Sally the news face-to-face. For a change we're not assaulted by Bunga as soon as we come in the door. Auntie Sally says Erika has taken him for a walk, but more likely it's vice versa given what I've seen of Bunga's leash training.

Usually Mom makes me go find Taylor when she wants

to have a serious conflab with Auntie Sally but today the news explodes out of her before I can clear the drama zone.

Unlike Mom, Auntie Sally is thrilled. She claps her hands to her cheeks and says, "Dad has a girlfriend? Wow!"

"I'm to make up only one bed," says Mom, wide-eyed with secret meaning that of course I understand.

Auntie Sally blinks. "They are adults, Ev," she says.

"Do you think Dad knows about STD's?" Mom says. "You know that AIDS is on the increase in Florida because seniors aren't taking precautions."

"I'll go find Taylor," I say.

I knock at Taylor's door and after a second or two she says, "Come in." When I open the door and she sees that it's me she slides a book on animal communication out from under her chemistry textbook. "I thought you were Mom," Taylor says. "She thinks I'm studying. Well, I am studying, but not what she thinks. Close the door and give me a few minutes here—I'm about to try something new."

Taylor returns to her reading. She is surrounded by angels, her new motif since purging her room of unicorns. There are angels on her wallpaper and on her fluffy bedspread. Being in Taylor's room is like being in heaven, with a couple of exceptions. There's a framed photo on each corner of her desk. At one side is Spike, looking very handsome in a long-eared sort of way. On the other side is Franco, glowering, lids half-closed, probably trying to look like a serious macho killing machine.

Taylor closes her eyes. I lean against the wall and wait. "I'm receiving a message from Spike," she says, patting her desk blindly for his picture then grasping it finally and pressing it to her chest.

I roll my eyes. It's safe, since Taylor is deep in trance and can't see me.

"He's on alert. There's a dog in the field. He says he's going to kill it."

I check to make sure she really has Spike's photo and hasn't grabbed Franco's by mistake. I remember what she told me before, about how donkeys can be used as livestock protection animals, and that one of them killed a cougar.

"Not Bernadette, I hope. Tell him not to stomp Kansas's puppy," I say.

Taylor communicates these instructions silently through the psychic universe, though I see her lips moving. "Spike says it's not Bernadette, it's a big brown stinky dog."

My breath catches in my chest. "How big?" I say.

"Spike says it's in the ditch at the far side of the pasture, so he can't tell for sure. But it's really big, the biggest dog he's ever seen—but he's not scared, not one bit. He has his herd to protect he says."

"Maybe it's a bear," I say, which is nothing more than pathetic wishful thinking. "Tell him to be careful." My heart is pounding. My cynicism has evaporated. I believe. How did this happen? How can I suddenly know with such certainty that my flakey cousin is in psychic communication with her hinny who is in pursuit of a sasquatch?

"Spike says it's not a bear, he knows what they smell like. He's only smelled a dog this bad a couple of times before, once when some dog named Bullet had rolled in something really dead where he lived back in Saskatchewan, and the other time was when we came out to meet you on that walk to the river. Stinky dog."

"Maybe we should phone Kansas and tell her to check the horses," I say, which shows how panicked I am because Kansas has no tolerance for fringy psychic stuff.

Taylor reaches blindly for her cellphone.

"No—wait!" I pounce on her hand, mashing it to the

desk. I've just imagined Kansas coming face to face with a sasquatch. Better for Spike to deal with it.

"It's leaving," says Taylor. "Spike says it crawled under the fence where it crosses the ditch. He says we should tell Kansas about this place, he says it's not safe, he's afraid Electra could get out this way too." Her eyes flutter open. "Oh that was exciting!" she says. "And I think Spike has a crush on Electra! Do you think it was a bear? Really? Or a stinky stinky dog?" She laughs. This has been a lark for her.

For me, it's been terrible. I don't want Spike to be hurt. I don't want the sasquatch to be hurt. I don't want Kansas to go into cardiac arrest. It's all so out of my control, I'm desperate to change the subject.

I don't even think first, I blurt out, "Grandpa's coming. Today. With his new girlfriend, Isobel. My mom's freaked because they only want one guest bed and she doesn't know if Isobel has had an AIDS test."

"Oh ick," says Taylor. "Definitely too much information." She returns Spike's framed photo to its place on her desk and considers it fondly. "He's fine now. He's eating grass."

I sigh, and relax immediately, as though I believe Taylor completely. Maybe she really can do this psychic animal communication thing. Maybe when she's more experienced she won't even need a photo, so if I described an animal to her and it was in the vicinity, she could make contact. Wouldn't it be amazing if she could communicate with a sasquatch. I wonder what Mr. Losino would make of that; probably not much, given that he is a scientist.

I flop onto Taylor's bed, lie on my back with my hands behind my head and contemplate the ceiling.

"I've decided to become a scientist when I grow up," I say, "like Mr. Losino."

Taylor swivels in her chair. "Mr. Losino isn't a scientist. He's some sort of egghead who works with computers. That's what Franco tells me. He says everyone in his family is an intellectual except him. No matter how much he tries, he can't come up to their expectations. It's very hard on his self-esteem. That's why he's decided to concentrate on developing his body instead of his brain."

I prop myself on one elbow and stare at Taylor, but am unable to speak. Obviously Franco has lied to her, and she'd be hurt if I told her so. On the other hand, she might take Franco's word over mine, then tell him what I said and he'd find me and kill me. I don't know what to do.

"What?" says Taylor. "You look like you've got a migraine, your eyes have gone all shifty."

"Oh…well," I say, scrambling for something, anything.

"You don't like him, do you. That's all right, nobody does, my mom won't even speak of him, I don't care. I'm the only one who really understands him." She swivels around so she can gaze at Franco's photograph. "I love him with all my heart."

I'm not good at these sorts of conversations, and any response that comes into my mind probably won't be the right thing to let out of my mouth, but still I find myself saying, "Sure Taylor, but why?"

She looks at me with exasperation, as though I've asked her why the sky is blue. She sighs as she draws on her stores of tolerance for the young and stupid. "Oh Sylvia. You don't ask questions like that. Love just is. When you've been in love some day you'll understand."

I sit up on the bed. Now I'm mad. I hate it when people talk to me like this, especially someone who's only one year ahead of me. "Yeah, but don't you need to *like* him too? What's to like about Franco?"

Taylor glares at me. "Franco's likable," she insists. After a few seconds she adds, "Physically he's very attractive."

I try not to choke. I try not to let the disgust show on my face, but I guess it does anyway because Taylor turns away and I can tell that she's hurt. I'm mad at myself for hurting her, and I'm mad at Taylor for being hurt, for after all I haven't said anything critical of her. Quite the opposite, it's because I think so highly of Taylor that I can't understand why she'd pair up with a lump like Franco.

She touches a fingertip to the glass over Franco's thin lips. "Plus I admire his dedication to sports, and how he takes good care of his body. It's not simple to get as strong as he is. He has to do research, and then he orders special nutritional supplements over the Internet." She pauses for a long time, so I almost believe she's completed the list of Franco's attributes, pathetic as it is. Then she says, "And he likes me." She says this as though it's the icing on the cake, the inarguable justification for her loving the big turkey.

I can't help myself—I'm enraged. "Of course he likes you!" I say. "You're totally likable. Only a moron wouldn't like you. If Franco liked someone like me it might be significant." I cringe inside. I hadn't meant to take the conversation this direction. It sounds like I'm feeling sorry for myself, and I'm not.

Of course Taylor takes it the wrong way. "Would you like him to like you?" she says. "Because I don't mind if you have a crush on him, I would totally understand."

"Are you kidding?" I say before I can stop myself. And before Taylor can figure out whether to be hurt again or not, I quickly add, "I'm scared of Franco. He's so big."

I've saved the day. Taylor smiles. "Franco's not scary. He's a big softy. I think he's like Spike. He's misunderstood and doesn't always fit in very well with others."

I will my eyes not to roll. It feels like they might fall out of my head with the effort. It's all I can do to not remind Taylor that Spike is part-donkey, yet another quality he has in common with Franco, but I figure Spike has been insulted enough.

"Besides," says Taylor, "don't you like Franco's brother Logan?"

Oh no. What have I started? I'm not ready to talk about this. I'm barely ready to think about it in the privacy of my own head.

Taylor says, "Franco's been really worried about Logan. Until you appeared on the scene he figured Logan was gay. He was sure the kids at school would find out and make Logan's life miserable."

"Really?" I say. "No one could make Logan's life miserable. He turns everything into a joke. Everybody likes him."

"There's another side to Franco. You should give him a chance," says Taylor.

I'm saved from having to respond by a light tapping at the door, and Mom saying, "Honey, we have to go. The frozen yoghurt will be melting in the car."

She doesn't need to convince me. I bolt from the bed, only pausing long enough before opening the door to give Taylor a chance to slide her chemistry text over top of the animal communication book. Maybe it's a good thing she's taken such an interest in animal communication. This must be what's given her the skill to communicate with a supplement-eating meatball like Franco.

But in the silence of the drive home, with Mom sniffing at the steering wheel and not wanting to talk for once in her life, I have the opportunity to reconsider my opinion. If Taylor is psychic, she may have sensed good things in Franco that a social misfit like me wouldn't notice in a million years.

And Taylor is such a wonderful kind person she will be a positive influence on him. Taylor will bring out the best in him.

She's right, I do need to give Franco a second chance.

# chapter eighteen

We have Chinese take-out for dinner. Isobel insisted, she didn't want any fuss or bother. She and Grandpa arrived at the door at five o'clock with two huge bags of the stuff. Fortunately Mom hadn't started her own preparations yet. She just said thank you then took the containers into the kitchen to stick in the oven to keep warm.

Now the dining room table is cluttered with cardboard boxes and aluminum trays.

"Dad, I didn't know you liked Chinese," says Mom as Grandpa loads up his plate.

"I didn't until Isobel came along. She showed me how to order the good stuff. Before that I never knew there was anything other than sweet and sour chicken balls."

Grandpa looks younger than last time I saw him a couple of months ago. He's less grey somehow. He smiles all the time and there's more colour in his cheeks. He's dressing better too. There's not a single stain on his shirt and he's wearing new pants that come all the way down to the top of his shoes so his bony ankles and white socks don't show when he walks.

"Don't you worry about the sodium and saturated fat

levels?" says Mom. I guess she hasn't noticed how much healthier Grandpa is looking.

"Isobel's the health and nutrition expert. I leave all that up to her," says Grandpa.

"You're a doctor?" says Dad.

"Oh no," says Isobel. "Doctors don't know anything about nutrition! I worked in the hospital kitchen in Regina for several years."

"She ran the whole place," says Grandpa.

"Oh, Henry, I did not," says Isobel. "And I'm retired now."

"Hospital Employees' Union member?" says Dad. "I suppose you're locked into an employee pension fund?"

"Tony!" says Mom.

"What?" says Dad. "I was only asking a question."

Grandpa says, "I met Isobel on the plane on my way home from my last visit here. She'd been staying with her son, taking care of him for a while after his marriage fell apart." He leans over and gives her a peck on the cheek, which I think is quite cute, but Mom looks away.

Isobel turns to Grandpa, dropping her chin so she can see over her glasses. She raises her eyebrows, which are not real but drawn on, which is pretty weird, but what really strikes me is how pointy her nose is. It's not so obvious from the front, but in profile, it's truly incredible. She must have been teased terribly when she was a kid.

Isobel pats Grandpa on the arm. "Easy there, Tiger," she says. "You control yourself in front of the children. And grandchild." She smiles in my direction, then looks back at Grandpa.

I think I like Isobel.

Grandpa growls at her. He's gone quite silly, though I suppose this is an improvement over how he was going before, which was downhill fast into senile dementia.

"Isobel saved my life," says Grandpa.

"Hardly that," says Isobel.

"You did!" says Grandpa. "I was growing old before my time. You were the one who suggested I have my testosterone levels checked."

"My first husband struggled terribly with andropause," Isobel explains to the rest of us.

"What?" says Dad.

"It's the male equivalent of the female menopause," says Isobel.

Grandpa drags his eyes off Isobel to include us all in his testimonial, whether we want to be or not. "Now I'm on the patch. Transdermal testosterone replacement therapy. Feel like my old self. I used the hormone cream from the compounding pharmacy for a while, but darned if Isobel wasn't contaminated somehow, and we couldn't have that could we?" He chuckles and gazes at Isobel the same way Kansas and Declan make puppy eyes at each other.

Mom squirms. Dad looks angry as usual. He used to have a more normal range of emotional responses; now he only has this one, so Mom and I live in a constant state of yellow alert. I wish there was a way of warning Grandpa and Isobel.

"I was irritable, my strength was going, I had no stamina, and little...er...appetite for...er...life," says Grandpa, glancing warily in my direction. I try to look like I don't know exactly what he's talking about even though, unfortunately, I do. Then it hits me like a freight train, how I've heard all this before.

"Just like Dad!" I say.

A great heavy silence descends upon the dining room table. Now what have I done? I've made this great discovery that explains everything and no one's happy about it.

"Oh good lord," says Mom eventually, her voice cracking.

"Mom?" I say. Why should she be on the verge of tears?

She doesn't look at me. She speaks as though to the chandelier over the table. "I thought it was something else, I thought there was something going on."

Isobel nods. "Most wives do," she says. "It can be a great relief, sidestepping all that blame, self-recrimination and guilt."

What are they talking about?

"My testosterone levels are fine," says Dad. There are veins showing on his forehead.

"No, wait Dad, remember how you got so mad you threw my bike across the yard, and you've had road-rage, and you said yourself you aren't so hungry at dinner, and your golf isn't going so well because you've lost your power on the fairways." I won't add the other thing, about no making up with Mom in the bedroom. I know better than to say that out loud, or even hint at it.

But I might as well have said it, I might as well have got it all off my chest and really stirred up the hornets nest, because Dad's eyes are shrinking back into his head. We've slipped past yellow and we're deep into amber alert. I steady myself on my chair. I weight my seat bones equally and stretch my back tall, just like I do on Brooklyn, even though last time I did this it only seemed to make Dad worse.

"It's a simple test," says Grandpa. "Your GP can order blood work. Or you can have a saliva test done through some pharmacies, that's what Isobel did."

"I didn't know I had so much spit in me," says Isobel, laughing. She's trying to divert Grandpa's attention, but he doesn't notice.

"You might be surprised," he tells Dad. "I've done lots

of research about it now. There are many men out there suffering needlessly with low testosterone levels. Including young fellas like you."

"Not me," says Dad.

Isobel reaches over and rubs Dad's arm. "I'm sure not," she says, but her tone says she doesn't believe him at all and that she understands he's not ready to know the truth yet.

This is not a good strategy to use with my dad.

He glares at Isobel's offending hand and drags his arm out of her reach. His fingers come to rest on his table knife. I so wish he'd used the little wooden chopsticks like the rest of us.

I have to do something before someone is killed.

"I saw a sasquatch, when I was out riding," I say.

Four pairs of eyes stare at me in another great silence that stretches on and on until Isobel coughs softly into her napkin.

Mom says, "Oh, Honey, I thought you'd outgrown this stage. Though I suppose some regression is understandable during family stress."

Isobel cocks her head and blinks at Mom as if she'd just spoken two lines of Martian.

Grandpa looks thoughtful.

Dad, of course, is angry. "Oh for god's sake, Sylvie. The sasquatch is a myth. There's no such thing. Just like UFOs."

"They're not a myth. Mr. Losino knows all about them—he's a wildlife biologist. And I saw one. You can't see myths," I say.

"There has been no evidence. Show me one body," says Dad.

"They're nocturnal," I say. "And intelligent. And shy. Mountain gorillas weren't discovered until 1902, and they can't run as fast as sasquatches."

Dad leans back in his chair and closes his eyes. I think he's counting to ten; I wish he'd shoot for a hundred—that might bring his blood pressure back under control.

I don't know what else to say. I stare at my placemat.

Grandpa says, "You know, Tony, Pipsqueak has a point here—just because a species hasn't been officially catalogued doesn't mean it can't exist."

"Stay out of this, Henry," says Dad. He stabs the tabletop between us repeatedly with an emphatic index finger. "Sylvia, you saw a bear. That's bad enough, that you came across one of those when you were out riding. What did Kansas do?" He picks up his knife and fork and attacks a chunk of pork on his plate.

I'm not going to tell him that Brooklyn and I were out on our own. I'm not going to get Kansas in trouble, and I'm not going to get myself in more trouble. I pull my lips tight against my teeth and don't answer.

Grandpa says, "I saw one once, crossing a harvested corn field. Scared the bejesus out of me. Must have been fifty years ago, but I'll never forget it."

Dad's knife and fork crash on his plate. He shoves back his chair and leaves the table. The chandelier makes happy tinkling noises when he slams the front door.

Isobel raises her painted eyebrows.

Mom struggles to retrieve a tissue from her pocket, but it comes out in long shreds. "Oh hell," she says, and departs for the kitchen.

"Henry, you haven't told me you saw a sasquatch," says Isobel.

"I stopped telling people a long time ago. Got nothing but ridicule. I suppose I put it out of my mind until Pips here reminded me," says Grandpa.

They're acting as though nothing has happened, as

though all our family drama is of no more significance than something on reality TV. Maybe they're right. It has nothing to do with them, they didn't do anything wrong, it's not their fault. I look from one of them to the other. Maybe it's not my fault either.

I say, "Mr. Losino wants me to take him to the place where I saw it. He's hoping there will be some tracks that he can cast. Or maybe he'll find some hair."

"For DNA analysis?" says Isobel.

"Only if a follicle is attached. Even then there are problems," I say. It's so nice to be taken seriously. It's great to be able to talk about everything I learned from Mr. Losino. I could give both of them such a big hug. "Would you like to come with us? It would be a long walk." I know they're old and maybe they can't walk all the way to the river, but I wouldn't mind going so much if more people were with me. "Mr. Losino wouldn't mind. And Logan would come too. Logan is my…" I can't say it out loud. I just can't.

"Friend?" says Isobel.

I sure hope Grandpa marries her, soon, before he dies.

# chapter
## nineteen

My dad and I are sitting alone at the dining room table. He's not talking, and he's wearing his predatory bird face. Clearly he's mad at me for something. I hear a tapping at the window and turn to see Brooklyn peering in at us. Ah—it's a dream. Brooklyn's wearing his bridle and saddle. He wants me to come out and go for a ride, which would be a much better dream than one where I'm sitting waiting for my dad to explode all over me.

I don't even bother to balance on my seat bones or sit tall. I just say, "Dad, I'm going for a ride on Brooklyn now," and get up from the table and walk out the door.

I know—this is totally unrealistic. But it's my dream, and I'm in charge.

The trouble is, when I get outside, there's no sign of Brooklyn on the lawn, so I won't be doing any riding. I consider the front door, and there's no way I'm going back inside. Only one option remains. I wake myself up.

I wish I'd had a more useful dream, because today I'm heading out on a sasquatch safari.

When Dad came back from his "walk" last night, Mom phoned Mr. Losino and gave permission for me to join him on an expedition, and Mr. Losino suggested we go out today. Mom told me I had to ask Kansas if it was okay that we went through her property. I didn't know what I would say to her because Mr. Losino wanted everything kept top secret outside of family. Fortunately I got Kansas's answering machine, and left a message that we were coming out for a hike, which wasn't even a lie.

Mr. Losino told my mom that anyone from my family was welcome to join us, so I'm taking Grandpa and Isobel, and I'm going to ride Brooklyn. Mom said she wanted to stay home for some quiet time. Dad said he didn't have time to go on wild goose chases, which is fine with me, I don't want him to come.

I'm all confused about my dad. Partly I know I'm feeling hurt because he was angry with me and didn't believe I saw a sasquatch. Mostly I'm upset that he's so adamant he doesn't have a hormone deficiency, as though it would be a shameful thing, while for months he and Mom have been telling me that my hormone deficiency is no big deal. He is such a hypocrite. Fine for me to have to take estrogen replacement therapy, but him taking testosterone is something totally different. He'll never get tested, I know he won't.

Grandpa's rental car is a Toyota Yaris and from the outside it looks really small, but once you get inside you can see how deceiving it is. There's tons of room in the back for me and all the extra stuff that Grandpa and Isobel say they have to bring, like slickers in case it rains, trekking poles for rough terrain, snacks for when their blood sugar gets low, changes of socks, changes of shoes, rain hats, sun hats, sunscreen, water bottles and a first aid kit from St. John Ambulance. I didn't know going for a walk was so complicated once you got old.

Grandpa and Isobel chatter back and forth to each other as we drive out to the barn, so from the back seat I can study Isobel's nose without her noticing. She must be self-conscious about it. I sure would be. I wonder why she never had plastic surgery. I wonder how she manages to kiss Grandpa without poking his eye out.

Grandpa says, "You're quiet back there, Pipsqueak. Got anything on your mind?"

"No, not really," I say. I'm sure not going to mention what I've been thinking about.

"Are you worried about your dad?" says Isobel.

"Worried? I don't think so," I say.

"You're probably angry with him," says Grandpa.

I think about that. It doesn't seem right to be angry with him. I'm supposed to love and respect him.

"Maybe just disappointed," says Isobel, turning to smile at me.

I nod, because this sounds about right. Disappointed is enough.

Grandpa and Isobel watch me ride Brooklyn in the ring until Logan and Mr. Losino arrive. Mr. Losino is driving an old yellow truck, or at least I think it's a truck. There's a sign on the door saying "Sasquatch Research." So much for top secret.

"Is that a Land Rover?" says Grandpa, full of admiration. "I haven't seen an old beauty like this for a coon's age."

Mr. Losino pats the hood affectionately, like I would pat a horse. "Yessiree," he says, "this old girl has seen lots of interesting country."

Kansas finally shows up, looking like she just got out of bed, though I know she hasn't because the horses were turned out when we got there and all the stalls had been cleaned. She's met my grandpa before, but I introduce her to everyone else. I tell her we're going on a sasquatch hunt and she doesn't even raise an eyebrow. This is so unlike her.

Logan climbs into the bed of the truck, lifts his bike over the side and lowers it gently to the ground. He warms up with some tricks. Obviously he's showing off, which is sweet, except that he sprays the gravel in the parking lot, and I make him rake it flat before Kansas says anything.

Mr. Losino tells Kansas that the very best way to spot sasquatches is from horseback, but Kansas says she doesn't run the sort of stable that has rental horses. Kansas doesn't want to come with us either. She says she isn't feeling well. Isobel suggests some ginger tea. I hope Kansas doesn't have some fatal disease, though if she did maybe I could run the stable for her until she died tragically and left everything to me in her will. Kansas shows me how to put the halter overtop of Brooklyn's bridle and tie the lead rope around his neck with a noose knot which I can undo and then tether him to a tree by the river if I need to.

Brooklyn likes following Logan on his bike. I have to keep asking Brooklyn to slow down, he actually draws close enough to breathe down Logan's neck. I think this makes Logan a bit scared, though he never says so, he just laughs and pedals faster.

Before we race too far ahead, Mr. Losino yells for us to wait, he doesn't want us to scare off the sasquatch, which reminds me why we're all here. I'd forgotten somehow, and I'm quite happy for the adults to catch up. Grandpa is breathing heavily so Isobel insists on taking the backpack. Mr. Losino already has one stuffed with all his scientific gear and a plastic bucket dangling off the back.

When we arrive at the river, there's no sasquatch at the far side, which frankly is a great relief to me. I point to the place where I saw it though, and Mr. Losino wades across in his gumboots, and then Grandpa and Isobel take off their shoes even though this means walking without their orthotics which for some reason is never supposed to happen. They act like a couple of kids being bad. Grandpa says, "I won't tell if you won't tell." And Isobel says she sure won't tell if Grandpa won't. Oh brother.

I take off Brooklyn's saddle so he doesn't rub it on a tree, then remove his bridle, slip the halter back on and tether him to an alder. When I'm finished, I see Logan hasn't crossed the river with everyone else. He's sitting on a boulder waiting for me.

I'm feeling more relaxed than last time I was here because Brooklyn has his head down eating grass, which means there isn't a sasquatch within a mile or two. I take a seat on a rock beside Logan. My rock is quite a bit taller so for once I can look Logan in the eyes without getting a kink in my neck, which is very nice. We both take off our helmets. Logan gives me a stick of gum. I catch a whiff of his medicated shampoo and move closer.

"I sure hope I haven't wasted everyone's time," I say. "Sometimes I think I imagined everything."

"You wouldn't do that," says Logan. "You don't make things up."

"Yes I do," I say. "I used to imagine you had a unicorn horn sticking out of your forehead. I thought that's why you wore a hat all the time when school started this year."

Logan snorts. "If only," he says. "Franco shaved my head in August. He said it would be less girly. I looked stupid."

"It's grown back very well," I say, peering closely. "And there's no sign of dandruff anywhere."

Logan blinks. "Thanks?" he says eventually.

"I used to think I was growing a horn too," I tell him. I flip over my helmet and show him where I carved out a space in the Styrofoam liner. I lift my bangs so he can see the lump on my forehead.

"That is so cool," he says. He runs a finger over the bump, down my nose and for a fraction of a second I feel his fingertip on my lips. Or maybe I imagined it. It was light as a feather, and scented like liniment.

I take his hand and hold it close to my nose and sniff. "What is that smell?" I say.

Logan flips his hand and curls his fingers around mine. "That'll be Franco's special macho sports skin tonic. He sprays some on my palms whenever he has the chance. He wants to make sure I don't turn gay."

"I wouldn't care if you were gay," I say, only because I know what it's like to be teased and bullied for being who you are.

"I know you wouldn't," says Logan. "But I'm not."

He squeezes my hand and holds it tight. Message received, and I'm swept into a panicky silence. We sit so quietly that I'm aware of Logan's pulse through my hand. I've never felt so close with someone in my life. I can feel his heart!

"I hope that special macho sports tonic doesn't make you turn out like Franco," I say. It's a weak joke, because I need to distract myself. I'm feeling excited and frightened at the same time. I hope Logan can't feel my pulse, which is hammering away like a rabbit's.

Logan laughs. "Are you kidding? Franco is such a bonehead he's probably spending a fortune on perfumed water. I'm not stupid, I wouldn't let him spray me if I thought it would actually do something to me."

"You are getting taller," I say, and then without thinking properly, "and you've started growing a mustache." I shouldn't have said this—what if Logan was self-conscious about the line of brown fluff on his upper lip?

"You noticed!" he says.

Good grief, he's proud of the thing.

He strokes the fringe of hairs with a fingertip like he's soothing a pet baby caterpillar. "I'll be trimming it pretty soon, it's not long enough yet. But this isn't from the sports spray. Remember what my mom told you—I'm a late bloomer, or at least I am in comparison to Franco. He started changing when he was about ten. He was shaving when he was thirteen, back when he still allowed me in the bathroom. Not that I'd want to spend time closed in a small room with him now— he's gone too crazy and he rages all the time."

"Maybe he's testosterone-deficient," I say. "That happened to my grandpa, and he says it might be why my dad is so irritable. My grandpa uses a testosterone patch." I stop because Logan is laughing.

"Oh yeah, you're so funny. I can just imagine asking Franco if maybe he's low on testosterone. He'd knock my head clear off with one of his fifty-pound weights."

To be polite I make some laughing noises, though something about this is bothering me.

Across the river, Mr. Losino is hunched over, peering at the ground as he works his way slowly down the sandy stretch near where I saw the sasquatch. Grandpa and Isobel are sitting close together on a big rock; I think they're doing pulse checks.

Logan drops my hand and unties his shoes. "Come on, Sylvia," he says. "Let's cross the river."

I raise my freed hand to my nose and catch a faint whiff of the tonic. "The thing is, Logan, this stuff doesn't smell perfume-y. It smells more medicinal. It reminds me of the liniment we use on the horses' legs sometimes, and Kansas always warns me about it and tells me not to use too much or it can burn, and I have to wear rubber gloves because she doesn't want me absorbing anything through my skin that hasn't been approved for human consumption by the Food and Drug Administration. Do you know anything about it or why Franco uses it? Have you ever read the ingredients on the label?"

Logan kicks off his shoes. "Franco says it helps him build muscles. He buys it off the Internet. He won't let me read the contents and he hides the bottle in his gym bag after he uses it. Which reminds me, it's supposed to be a big secret. Franco made me promise not to tell anyone about it. So don't say anything or he'll kill us both."

Of course I nod my head in agreement, the last thing I want to do is make Franco angry. Plus I like having a secret with Logan. Then another possibility occurs to me and I say, "You don't suppose it's an illegal drug, do you? Like the stuff Olympic athletes use until it shows up in their urine tests?"

"I don't know," says Logan, peeling off his socks. "I figured it was something harmless, like some Chinese herbal thing."

"It's not harmless if it's made by poachers from the parts of endangered wild animals," I say.

There are short black hairs poking through the skin on the top of Logan's big toe, and a line of hairs along the ridge of his foot.

"Oh," says Logan. "You're right. I hadn't thought of that."

"Maybe it's made from ground up sasquatch hair," I say. "Maybe that's why almost all the sasquatches disappeared. They've been poached for the Chinese traditional medicine industry, like the white rhinos and the mountain gorillas in Africa."

"Hey!" shouts Mr. Losino from across the river. "We found something! A footprint!"

# chapter
## twenty

Mr. Losino takes several photographs of the footprint and then makes a plaster cast and writes lots of notes in his journal. He says it's a fantastic find. He's really excited, like a little kid. I can imagine him celebrating tonight with even more secret chocolate sauce on his ice cream.

I shouldn't make fun, because Mr. Losino says this is serious science and we have made a significant contribution with our discovery. He's so pleased that he's not at all disappointed that we didn't see an actual sasquatch. I'm not disappointed either; the footprint is enough to prove that I wasn't imagining anything, or even confusing what I saw with a bear—the footprint is nothing at all like a bear track, Mr. Losino showed us comparative drawings in his field book.

The person who is disappointed is Grandpa. He scans the forest beyond the river and sighs. "I wanted to see another one before I die," he says.

"You have lots of time," says Isobel.

Mr. Losino is rinsing his bucket in the river; he stands up so fast that he drops the handle and almost loses the bucket in the current. "Another sasquatch? You've seen one before, Henry?"

"It was a long time ago," says Grandpa. "I was a boy, not much older than Logan. The memory has stayed with me my whole life."

"That's understandable," says Mr. Losino. "I'm still hoping to see one. Now that will be a day for celebration!"

Logan isn't paying much attention. He's squatting, staring at the cast drying in the sand, and he's looking sad. Logan never looks sad. He's always happy and joking around. It tears my heart out to see him like this. I crouch beside him. "Are you disappointed?" I ask him. "Because we can come here another time, and maybe the sasquatch will be back."

Logan is drawing squiggly lines with a stick in the sand beside the cast. "I'm a little disappointed I guess. But something else bothering me." He swivels on his heels so his back is to Mr. Losino and drops his voice to a shade over a whisper. "All these years my dad's been obsessed with sasquatches, and I never really believed him one hundred percent. I went along with his stories, because they made him so happy and he was so enthusiastic. In the back of my mind I always wondered if he was like those crazy people building landing platforms for alien spaceships. Plus Franco said he was nuts, and wouldn't let me tell anyone at school. I wasn't even supposed to tell you that my dad is a biologist because Franco tells everyone he's a computer nerd. That's why he wouldn't let you keep your bike in our garage too, because Franco didn't want you to see the Land Rover. Franco only worries about himself and his own reputation, but I gave in to him and was disloyal to my dad. And now I see," he says, pointing to the footprint, "that he was right all along. I feel like I've been a bad son."

I don't know what to say. I'm not used to people confessing personal things to me, being the social outcast that I am. My mom would have something to say, probably about sibling rivalry, that would make me want to stuff a sock in her mouth. When Brooklyn's upset mostly I stroke his neck. I look up at Logan's neck, sticking white and bare out of the band of his T-shirt, tendons popping, Adam's apple bobbing. It's not nearly as appealing as Brooklyn's fur-covered expanse of smooth muscle. No way I'm rubbing Logan's neck. But my hand creeps out, as if on it's own mission, and finds Logan's forearm, and rubs it gently back and forth. I can feel the hair on his arm and the warmth of his skin. I tell him what I tell Brooklyn.

"It's okay," I say.

He looks down at me and smiles. Then he takes on a very serious expression with a heavy frown, and squinty eyes, so I know everything's back to normal because he's going to come up with one of his corny jokes. "I guess anything I do is an improvement on Francopithecus," he says.

Mr. Losino says we'll have to wait for almost an hour for the plaster to cure. Fortunately Grandpa and Isobel have brought lots of heart-friendly nutritional snacks so none of us will starve. I wade back through the river to rescue Brooklyn who's eaten all the grass within reach. Logan stays behind because he wants to help his dad, which is pretty nice.

I strap on my helmet, lead Brooklyn to a fallen tree that I use as a mounting block and before anyone can stop me from riding bareback outside the riding arena, I boost myself up onto his back.

I use the lead-rope on one side of his neck, which makes steering more than the usual challenge, but Brooklyn is keen to do whatever I want.

There is nothing in the world that's as good as riding bareback on a fine horse like Brooklyn. I weave a chunk of his mane around my fingers and settle my bum on his soft warm back. Using my legs, I guide him into the river.

He likes it! He paws at the water until we're both soaked from splashes. He steps in farther and my bare feet submerge, then Brooklyn launches himself into the deeper part of the river and we're swimming! It's cold as ice, but oh boy is it fun! It's like riding a rocking horse, he goes up and down, and I can hear Grandpa applauding from the shoreline as we head out farther into the pool. This is better than anything I've ever imagined. It's even better than all my old dreams of riding.

The pool curves off to the left, and Brooklyn paddles across it until his front feet find the bottom at a narrow beach below a steep embankment. He clambers out of the water, shakes himself like a dog and I almost fall off, then he reaches down to graze on some coarse grass growing at the edge of the stones. When I recover my balance, I have a good look around. The curve in the river hides the scientific expedition from my line of sight. The bank in front of me must be a couple of metres tall, so sitting on Brooklyn's back I can barely see over it. There's a tangle of Oregon grape on the top, and beyond that, the cool mysterious darkness of a forest of mature fir trees.

It takes a moment for me to realize that Brooklyn and I are not alone.

About ten metres inside the forest, leaning against a tree, is the creature my dad insists does not exist: a sasquatch.

Brooklyn hasn't seen it, or smelled it apparently. Through my legs I can still feel that he's puffing from the effort of his swim, and his head is down searching for grass. If he brings it up and spies the sasquatch, I'm done for. He'll wheel away and I don't know if I can stay with him without saddle or bridle.

I stare at the sasquatch and it stares at me.

I know I need to stay calm. If Brooklyn senses that I'm alarmed, he'll go on alert and bring his head up. Kansas tells me that horses can feel our heartbeats even better than we can feel theirs. I consciously slow my breathing.

I know if I call back to everybody in the expedition party, the sasquatch will disappear into the woods as though it never existed.

It does exist.

They haven't all been destroyed in support of the traditional Chinese remedy industry.

I wonder what I can do, what sign I can make that won't be interpreted as threatening. Would a smile be too much like bared teeth? Would an arm-wave be aggressive?

I gradually raise one hand in front of me, the other one still clutching Brooklyn's mane. I have my palm forward, and twinkle my fingers, and say hi very very quietly.

The sasquatch doesn't move. Brooklyn shifts beneath me, stretching forward for more grass.

I must stay calm. I must observe as much as I can so I can report back to Mr. Losino with scientific accuracy.

I remember how Taylor calmed me after the last time I saw the sasquatch.

I take a deep breath, and quietly sing that corny song, the one about the hills being alive with the sound of music. As I sing, I grow aware of how appropriate the song is. The hills *are* alive, and with more than music. The world is alive with more wonders than we know.

For the sasquatch is a beautiful thing, with thick dark hair and big round eyes that stare and stare, as if trying to make sense of me and the squeaky sounds that emerge from my throat. It's not the same one as I saw before. I can't see breasts, this must be a male, though the long hair makes a definite identification impossible I'm not sorry to say. He is taller though, and his head has the same elongated shape as a male gorilla.

He continues to lean on the tree and consider me.

I square my shoulders and lift my sternum and relax my jaw. "With songs they have sung for a million years," I warble, the altered lyrics slipping out inadvertently, but this is the feeling the creature gives me, that he and his kind have been around for eons, inhabiting the forest, fishing in the rivers, leaning on the trees, watching us from the darkness.

Brooklyn lurches beneath me as he takes a step forward for more grass. I look down for no more than a second, and when I look up, the sasquatch is gone. There is no sound from his footfalls, no shrubbery waving in his wake. It's as though he was never there.

I tug on Brooklyn's lead rope until he lifts his head. He starts to take some interest in the space at the top of the bank, and he raises his nose for a better sniff of the air, but I plant my heels in his sides and pull again on the rope so he wheels and plunges again into the river for the swim back to the rest of the hunting party.

As we round the corner, I see Logan watching for me. They've finished with the casting and are back on the other side of the river packing up the gear.

For reasons I don't understand, I am breathless and shivering and sobbing when I reach them. I slide off Brooklyn but won't let go of his lead rope. Grandpa thinks I'm frightened and hypothermic, and he wants to wrap me in a special blanket from his first aid kit that looks like it's made from aluminum foil but Brooklyn won't let him near us with the crinkling flappy thing. So Isobel gives me her fleecy which she says will be better anyway because it will wick away some of the water. Logan holds my free hand,

and Mr. Losino peers at me and I wish I could talk but I can't.

One thing I know for sure is that I'm not frightened.

The world has become suddenly larger, and I can't describe how exciting I find this. I am overwhelmed with awe and wonder.

"Are you okay, Pipsqueak?" says Grandpa.

I nod and shudder with some more huge sobs that I really wish would go away.

"Take a deep breath," says Isobel.

I breathe. I lean against Brooklyn and draw air into my lungs and look away from the concerned people staring down at me. I watch the river sweeping past, all that water going somewhere. For a moment I am pulled by a sense of belonging and feel more connected to that river and to all things wild than I do to the cluster of humans around me. Logan squeezes my hand and brings me back. These are my friends. They care about me, and the river does not.

Isobel rubs my shoulders and the shivering subsides. Finally I am able to talk.

I look Mr. Losino in the eye. "I saw another one," I say. "I sang to him, and then he disappeared."

## chapter
### twenty-one

It's five o'clock by the time we arrive back at the stable and put Brooklyn away in his stall and pack up the car and load Logan's bike and Mr. Losino's equipment in the Land Rover.

Grandpa wants to invite Logan and Mr. Losino to join us for dinner at Auntie Sally's, but they say they have to get home, Mrs. Losino will have dinner waiting for them. Mr. Losino gives me a big hug before he leaves and tells me I'm a very lucky person. He hopes I can find time tonight to make some notes and sketches of what I saw and bring them to his house sometime soon. He says I can bring my dad if I want.

When Mr. Losino stops hugging me, Logan takes my fingertips in his and looks at me awkwardly and then he hugs me too. Even though Mr. Losino is more padded and comfortable for hugging, and he hugged me for longer, the brief embrace from Logan is more startling and gives me a fresh chill up my spine almost like the sensation I experienced from seeing the sasquatch.

Grandpa drives us to Auntie Sally's because we're due there by five-thirty, and he says there's no point in going back to my house first. He says Auntie Sally will have some clean dry clothes for me, as though this is some easy thing, as though my clothes are simply interchangeable with my cousins'. Even Erika is two sizes bigger than me, and she's only ten. Plus she's really into sequins, all of her clothes are covered with the things, you almost need sunglasses when she comes into a room, she's reflecting so much light. I'd rather freeze to death.

Dad's SUV is in the driveway already. I can hear Bunga barking in the backyard.

We sit in the car for a minute, as though none of us is quite ready to re-enter the real world of family life. I wouldn't mind some time on my own to think about what happened today. Seeing the second sasquatch has left me feeling disconnected from the world, as though I've entered an alternate universe I didn't know existed. I can't put better words to it than that, and don't know how I'm going to talk to people about it. Mr. Losino still recommends that I be cautious about who I tell. He didn't say to keep it secret from my family of course, but he insists I be careful at school. It's nice that he thinks he has to warn me about chatting at school, as though I'm normal, with a gaggle of girlfriends that I confide to.

Grandpa removes the key from the ignition and clears his throat. "Do we talk about this?" he says.

I say, "My mom doesn't approve of family secrets. She says they're pathological and toxic."

Isobel swivels in her seat to look at me. "I think this is more a matter of timing," she says. "I think it's a question of *when* to tell, not *if* to tell. Would tonight be the best time to be talking about sasquatches? It might be enough that Sally and her girls have to get used to the idea of their father and grandfather having a girlfriend."

"Only one miraculous news event at a time," says Grandpa.

Isobel pats him on the arm and smiles.

"If it was up to me, I'd prefer we not do anything tonight that might light my dad's short fuse again," I say.

"Very good point," says Grandpa. "Can we agree? Mum's the word on the sasquatch sighting? If asked, we had a great hike?"

I say okay, though I'm not sure about deceiving my parents, even if it is for a good reason.

"Isobel?" says Grandpa.

Isobel is cleaning some invisible dirt from under her thumbnail. Finally she looks to Grandpa, then to me and says, "Okay, but no lying. If asked a direct question, the truth comes out, bad timing or not."

This makes me feel much better, and Grandpa agrees too. He tells me not to worry, that he can deal with my dad. He says it like this is no big deal, as though he handles atomic explosions every day of his life. I wish someone would teach me how to do this.

Auntie Sally greets us at the door. She hugs Isobel even though it looks to me that Isobel was only going in close for a handshake. I hope Auntie Sally doesn't start calling her Mom right away. She can be pretty enthusiastic at times, and I don't want her setting precedents: I like Isobel well enough but don't know about calling her Grandma quite yet.

I lead the way into the living room where Mom and Dad are sitting close together on the couch, which at first I take to be a good thing, but then I notice they're in the midst of one of their low-volume high-octane arguments. Mom's lips are tight as a snake's and Dad's eyes are so squinty his eyeballs have disappeared.

When they see us, Mom and Dad try to look normal, and maybe they can fool everyone else but they can't fool me. To make things worse, I hear the slap of the dog door in the kitchen, and suddenly Bunga is in the room yelping and jumping all over us and then he humps Isobel's leg. Bunga is getting way worse as he ages. Mom says he's lost his impulse control and Dad says he can't lose what he never had. Auntie Sally gets all embarrassed and tells Erika to put Bunga in her bedroom. Erika says that Bunga was only showing how much he likes Isobel, but she packs him off to her bedroom as instructed and doesn't come back. I suppose she's locked herself in there with him, keeping him company. I don't think she's making a very good impression, but then I didn't really expect her to.

My mom tells me I need to clean up before dinner, as if I don't know that already. She says I look even more like a barn rat than I usually do when I come back from riding, which I take as a compliment even though I'm sure it wasn't meant as one.

I knock on Erika's door but she doesn't answer, which suits me fine, I didn't want her clothes anyway. Taylor's door is open but she's not there. I take a sweat suit out of her bottom dresser drawer. I have to dig deep to find something that isn't floral or pink. I lift out a set of old grey sweats that probably once belonged to Stephanie before she went off to university and my fingers catch in a sheet of paper tucked underneath. I try not to read it. I try to refold it and stick it back in the drawer, but my eyes betray me. It's a love letter, signed by Franco. Oh yuck, I wish I didn't know.

I dash from Taylor's bedroom, clutching her clothes, and scurry down the hall to the bathroom. I'm so distracted—by the love letter, by the sasquatch—that I ignore the closed bathroom door and walk in without knocking, and there's Taylor, perched on the edge of the bathtub, rinsing her calf with the hand-held shower head. She's been shaving her legs.

She looks up, her face in a fury, and I figure I'm going to die, but then she says, "Oh it's you. Shut the door quick! And lock it behind you. I don't want Erika in here, or Mom."

She holds the razor under the running water. The handle is contoured and pink. It's plastic shell packaging lies mangled on the floor beside the bath mat.

Taylor sniffs loudly and rubs her eye with the back of her wrist. "Mom says leg hair is natural and nothing to be ashamed of, but this is getting ridiculous." There's a tremor in her voice. She gestures disgustedly to her unshaven leg, the one that still has a big toe. The other foot she tucks underneath so I can't see it. She's still embarrassed by her amputation, which I don't understand, but don't have the time to dwell on it because I'm so taken with all the hair on her unshaven leg. She's as hairy as Logan Losino. She even has hair on the top of her foot like Logan does. She sure wasn't this way last summer when I saw her running around in shorts. Given the freshly unpacked shaving equipment, she wasn't defoliating then either.

"What's going on?" I say.

"I'm getting hair everywhere. And I mean *everywhere*," she says, making bug eyes. "Don't ask to see it, this is bad enough. Look at my arms! I look like a frigging monkey."

"Or a sasquatch," I say, because she does.

"Thanks a lot," says Taylor. "This is not a time for jokes, Sylvia." She runs some water, takes the bar of soap from its dish and lathers her leg.

"Sorry," I say. "It's just that…" I stop myself, because this probably isn't the best time to be talking to Taylor about my amazing sasquatch sightings and my new expanded universe. Probably there will never be a right time, Taylor would never take Spike for a walk again if she knew what creatures were lurking in the woods. Telling her about sasquatches could ruin her life.

"My life is ruined," says Taylor, as though she can read my mind, as though she's getting so good at this psychic communication stuff she doesn't even need to try any more or put herself in a spiritual frame of mind. She sure doesn't look spiritual right now. She swipes at her leg with the razor then holds it under the faucet again. "The stupid blades clog up in two seconds," she says.

I mentally review what I know about the growth of body hair in adolescence, which is quite a lot thanks to my mom's lectures and all the reading material she's provided. Taylor is almost sixteen, which seems late for changes like this. "I don't get it," I say. "You weren't...um...like this last summer."

"Of course I wasn't like this! I've never been like this. I'm not supposed to be like this. Mom isn't and Stephanie isn't. I've got man hair. It's so disgusting."

I'm about to make a wise crack about the hazards of hanging around with an ape like Franco, and stop myself just in time. It gets me thinking—about Logan's sudden late blooming, about the lingering smell of Franco's mystery sports tonic on my hands, about Isobel being contaminated by Grandpa's transdermal testosterone medication. I look at Taylor, who is probably my best friend, and I wouldn't care if she turned into a sasquatch, I would love her anyway, but I know she would hate herself. I have to do something to help her, even though it means betraying the secret that Logan asked me to keep, and puts me and Logan at risk of being killed by Franco.

I hand Taylor some toilet paper to stem the flow of blood from a nick on her ankle. "Apply pressure," I say. While we wait for the blot to clot, I tell her my theory that she's been contaminated by something in Franco's sports tonic.

"What sports tonic?" she says.

Oh boy. Some relationship they have.

"You know how Franco always smells kind of like Absorbine Senior horse liniment?" I say.

"You mean his aftershave?" says Taylor.

"It's not aftershave. It's a sports tonic he orders off the Internet to help him build muscles. He makes Logan use it so he doesn't turn into a homosexual. Logan's getting hairier too, though of course he likes it and thinks he's finally developing normally."

Taylor stares at me in horror. "I'm being turned into a man? Is there an antidote?" She drops the razor and clasps her head in her hands. The patch of toilet paper falls away and her leg starts bleeding again, a tiny rivulet that runs down over her heel and turns pink in the bottom of the tub.

"We have to find out what's in that spray," I say. "Franco keeps it top secret. He won't let Logan read the ingredients, and no one is supposed to know about it. He hides it in his gym bag."

"What if it is testosterone?" says Taylor. "Can I turn back into a woman if I stop being exposed to it?"

"I don't know. You could ask Grandpa's girlfriend. And you could do a saliva test."

Taylor's eyes are huge. "Maybe I should. If I could have a test and find out what's happening, that would be good. I wouldn't have to accuse Franco of anything. I know I told you he's a puppy dog, but he can be growly sometimes. And I wouldn't want to get him into any more trouble, or have him find me snooping through his gym bag." She pauses, thinking. "He has a lock on it, you know. I always thought that was strange, that he would bother to put a lock on a zipper on a canvas bag. At first I thought he did drugs, but he hates that stuff. He won't touch anything that might interfere with his athletic performance."

"Another kind of drug," I say.

Taylor sniffs, and nods.

We develop a scheme for steering the conversation at dinner so we can learn about saliva testing, which turns out to be much easier than we expected. Grandpa and Isobel are keen to provide details, though my mom and Auntie Sally exchange uncomfortable glances and Dad leaves the table because he says his BlackBerry is vibrating and Erika secretly slips her iPod bud in her ear and goes off to another universe altogether.

# chapter
## twenty-two

After dinner, when the conversation has shifted to a stupe-fyingly boring discussion comparing cruise lines to Alaska, Taylor and I escape back to her room.

"Did you see her nose?" says Taylor, which is surprising because Taylor is usually too spiritual for catty comments, but then I see she isn't being critical, she's amazed, like I used to be.

"I don't even notice it anymore," I say, because I don't. It's just Isobel.

Taylor takes a seat at her desk and I perch on the corner. In the glow from the computer screen I am alarmed to see a faint line of fuzz across her upper lip. Poor Taylor. She's living my nightmare, the one where I was growing facial hair. This is really weird. I hope I'm not responsible somehow, I hope this isn't yet another affliction I have accidentally foisted on my cousin.

Taylor does a web search and finds a place on the Internet where we can order and prepay a saliva test for hormones. It's expensive, especially since Taylor ticks off the overnight courier option. Taylor has her mom's MasterCard information from the last time they ordered home decorating books off Amazon.

"Isn't that stealing?" I say.

"No, it's a medical emergency," says Taylor. "There's no way I'm going to a local compounding pharmacy for a saliva test. Someone's bound to see me and report back, either to my mom or, worse still, to Franco."

I think about asking Taylor to order two extra sets, one for me and one for my dad. It looks like Isobel's right, you have to provide lots of saliva, and I don't see how I could get that much spit out of my dad without explaining myself. And I'm not nearly as hairy as Taylor, at least not yet anyway. Besides, I'd rather spend my money on a new bridle for Brooklyn. So the one test kit will have to do.

"What if it's delivered while you're at school?" I ask.

"I can't take that chance," says Taylor. "I'll have to fake a migraine and stay home."

"How long does a migraine last?"

"As long as I need it to," says Taylor. "This one could last a long time. Maybe a lifetime. I can't go to school like this. I can't shave everywhere. Look, I'm even growing a mustache!"

I peer at her lip and pretend to be surprised.

"The only reason Mom hasn't noticed is because she needs new glasses," says Taylor.

I want to help her, but don't have many words of advice. I wish I was more like my mom, who always has some advice handy, not that it's necessarily good, but it's better than this helpless silence. I put my hand on Taylor's arm and say, "Kansas tells me that when in doubt, just like with riding, you go forward."

"Go forward?" says Taylor. "What the hell does that mean?"

Now that she's asked me to explain, I realize I don't have a clue, and even when I think hard about it I can't see how this advice applies to Taylor's situation, but I muddle on anyway because Taylor needs my help, there's nobody else. "If you're going forward, your horse can't buck you off so easily, that's what Kansas means," I say.

Taylor says, "Well, my mom tells me that when in doubt—don't. That would be like not going forward, wouldn't it? Like maybe I should sit back and take stock of my situation for a while?"

This is getting way beyond confusing for me. If there's a catchy little phrase for each possible option, how do people make the right decisions? I don't know what to say.

Taylor swivels away from the screen so her back is towards me. She continues talking but I don't know if she's talking to me or herself or the dark space under her bed, which is the direction she is looking. "I know Franco didn't mean to do this, I know it was an accident, he would never do anything intentionally to hurt me. So I can't stop loving him for this, for a mistake. But I don't know if I want to call him, or if I want to see him, and if I do see him how do I stop him from touching me and increasing the contamination? Plus I'm afraid to keep shaving because I've heard this can make hair even coarser, but I'm afraid not to shave because I don't want anyone to see. My life is so over."

She sniffs loudly. I hand her a tissue. I place my hand on her back and awkwardly rub across her lumpy vertebrae and shoulder blades. In a way, there is not much to Taylor, a thin layer of skin and muscle over bones, the opposite of Brooklyn or Spike, or even Franco I suppose. She is fragile, and indescribably precious to me, and even if right now I don't have a clue how to help her, I know I'll figure out something.

That night I dream about Mr. and Mrs. Sasquatch. They

are swimming like dolphins in the deep part of the river. Okay, they're large hairy dolphins, but equally at home in the water. They stay underwater for incredible lengths of time, then reappear way across the pool, sometimes with a salmon in their hands.

Mr. and Mrs. S see me and beckon for me to join them. I'm riding Brooklyn, bareback again, but this time he's not concerned about the sasquatches, and plunges into the river and we swim with them. I would hardly know it was a dream, except that I'm not freezing to death or soaked to the skin.

On the riverbank, watching us, I see Taylor. She's so covered with hair she could almost be a baby sasquatch. She's crying. Somehow I know it's because she's lonely. Seeing Taylor like this makes me want to cry too, despite the fun that Brooklyn and I and the sasquatches are having.

Taylor pulls at her arm hair, then buries her face in her hands.

I look down at my own body, covered only with a transparent wet T-shirt. No hair. No nothing. I lift the hem of the shirt. Brooklyn hair, that's all.

Instead of relief, I feel disappointment. As gross as hair can be, it's also normal, and I'm not. I'm a Turner girl, and always will be.

Brooklyn clambers onto the beach and shakes himself like a dog so I have to throw my arms around his great warm neck to steady myself, and I wake up, wrapped around my pillow, feeling happy and sad at the same time.

It's still the middle of the night. The house is quiet, my clock radio glows red saying 2:22. I grab my flashlight and pull the covers over my head, and examine my sexless little body. The tiny hairs light up all over the place, and I have to admit that they've probably always been there, it's normal body hair that everybody has but mostly you can't see it unless you look very closely. I shine the light across my arm and then across my belly. I contort myself so I can check for hair on the top of my feet, in case it's transformed from my usual fuzz to that coarse dark hair that Logan and Taylor both have. It's the same as ever and I start to straighten myself out again, and the flashlight swings up past my thighs, and that's when I see it. I have a hair. One dark hair. I give it a gentle tug just in case it's lying there on the surface, unattached. My skin tents up at the base of the hair.

I am growing a dark hair.

Ohmygod I may need a bikini wax.

I'm so excited that I could scream, which I mustn't do because everyone is sleeping, so I bite the bed sheet instead.

Here I've been thinking that body hair is gross and I've been telling myself that I'm glad to not be developing or turning into a normal girl like Amber or Topaz but now I have a hair! And I'm ecstatic! Hair isn't nearly so gross when it's your own! I guess I've only been thinking it's awful because I figured I wasn't going to grow any. Maybe I'm a late bloomer too, maybe the Turner Syndrome has nothing to do with it.

I check my armpits. Nothing there. Oh well, it's a start.

I want to phone Taylor. But it's 2:25. And she wouldn't understand, not in her condition she wouldn't.

I lie in bed and remember my dream. I never think of Taylor as being lonely. She has a fan club at school, though of course that may only be due to her being an exotic amputee. At home she has three sisters, and Auntie Sally who probably doesn't count. And she has Bunga, and Spike, and me, and Kansas more-or-less, as Kansas doesn't seem to be available to any of us except Declan nowadays. And I hate to include him, but she does have that dope Franco.

Not that he's done her much good if he's contaminated her with his sports spray and given her man hair.

Oh. My spirits sink. Of course. The sports spray. That will be the source of my hair too. It had nothing to do with my becoming normal. I've been contaminated too, though for me it isn't a bad thing like it is for Taylor.

I can't allow Taylor to suffer any longer, not knowing. I have to find out what's in the tonic.

I think about enlisting Logan's assistance, but it's too dangerous for him. Franco would kill him, and I can't risk that.

It's nice thinking about Logan and feeling protective of him. It makes me feel warm and cuddly all over and I fall back to sleep.

# chapter
## twenty-three

I need a plan, and I can't think of one, even though I have the kitchen all to myself in the morning. I know that Grandpa and Isobel need lots of sleep because they're old and wearing out, plus no doubt exhausted from yesterday's hiking and wading in the river. I hope they haven't died in their sleep from overexertion. Dad says when you're old anything can happen at any time.

For a while I figure that Dad's up and gone to work already, but after I've finished my muesli I hear low voices from Mom and Dad's bedroom. I decide to leave for school before they start shouting again.

I'm in such a hurry, I don't even check the time, and when I arrive at Logan's house he's not waiting for me, and I see by my watch that I'm twenty minutes early. I stash Pinky in the shed, and I'm standing there admiring Logan's bike when Franco walks in. I can smell him before I see him, reeking of liniment, or whatever it is.

The amazing thing is that he's big and he's hairy but he's nowhere near as big and hairy as a male sasquatch, so I don't find him so scary anymore.

He looks sad. Or worried. Or sad and worried. Or maybe

mad. I don't know—I'm not very good at this, being a social isolate.

"Hey," he says.

I say hey back.

"You're Taylor's cousin, right?"

Oh boy. Some people are such slow learners. I tell him he's right, I'm Taylor's cousin.

"She sent me a text. She says she can't see me for a while."

"Oh," I say.

"Is she sick? Does she have swine flu? I need her." He collapses into a plastic garden chair in the corner of the shed. I'm surprised the chair doesn't break on impact; the legs wobble for a couple of seconds as Franco leans forward, plants his elbows on his knees and buries his head in his hands. "I can't believe this is happening to me," he mumbles.

What can I say? I don't want to break any confidences, not those of Taylor or Logan. Though right now Franco seems as threatening as a garden slug.

His great shoulders slump. His thick neck looks like it can no longer support his head. I'm almost ready to feel sorry for him when he sighs, sits back in the chair, slides out one foot and kicks his toe against Pinky's front tire. "So why do you leave this here anyway?" he says. "Why not ride it to school?"

"It's pink," I say.

"So?" says Franco.

"I'm not a girly-girl—as I think you've noticed. They'd tease me."

"I wear pink sometimes," says Franco. "So does Arnold Schwarzenegger."

"That's different," I say. "No one would tease you or Arnold. No one's going to question your masculinity, no matter what you wear."

Franco snorts. "That's true," he says.

And don't ask me why, or maybe he's sounding too smug, but I say, "Except maybe sequins. I don't think you could wear those."

He looks at me with his small dark eyes, checking that I'm not mocking him. I put on my most innocent expression, the one I usually save for dangerous encounters with my parents. Satisfied, he returns his attention to Pinky.

"I thought about repainting it," I say.

"It'd look like hell," says Franco, "unless you sanded down the frame and did it properly."

"That's what I was afraid of," I say.

"It would be better without the white handgrips and white seat," says Franco.

He's right. I can see it. All I'd need is black handgrips and a black seat. I can imagine my bike looking like something I could ride to school again, though of course I'd miss my walks back and forth with Logan, but on the other hand I'd have more time at the barn, and maybe I could meet Logan on other occasions, like for sasquatch searches.

I see something else—a glimmer perhaps of what Taylor sees in Franco. It's not a softness, like I felt when I changed the spelling of his name from Franko, and it's not just that he's being useful to me by helping with my bike dilemma. It's something different, which I don't understand let alone approve of, but for some reason I feel excitement at being so close to someone who could be so dangerous. Here I am, little old me, without a plan, winging it and feeling…great. I feel great.

"Taylor can't see you because she isn't well," I tell him.

"I knew it!" says Franco. "She couldn't break up with me!"

He sounds so relieved it's hard for me to tell him the

rest. I don't want to hurt his feelings, not really. It's like I'm testing myself, I feel like a lion-tamer, alone in a cage with a slightly domesticated wild animal and I say, "Franco, she could break up with you." When he looks at me with scornful disbelief, I say, "What's in your sports tonic, Franco? I've smelled it on her. I think she's having a reaction to it."

He's expressionless as he considers this information. Brooklyn can do the same thing when I give him an aid and he's not sure what to do about it. Kansas has coached me to be patient. So I wait.

"No way," he says eventually, but he drops eye contact, and his right hand slides to protect the front pocket of his jeans.

"Let me see the bottle, Franco. She's having a reaction to something. It could even be a good thing if it's your sports tonic, because maybe it will be reversible when she stops being exposed and she'll be well and she'll be able to see you again. Otherwise, she has to wait for tests..."

"Tests?" says Franco.

"She's going to have her saliva tested," I say.

"Oh no," says Franco. He moans, takes his head in his hands and lurches to his feet. I back towards the doorway. Franco walks around the shed in tiny circles until he bumps into Pinky. "Taylor can't do this to me," he says. He picks up Pinky, and I think my bike is going to have another flying lesson, like my old bike had from my dad, so using my best animal-training voice, I tell Franco to stop.

He catches himself. He has the bike at chest height, and he lowers it gently to the ground.

I lift my collarbones. "Let me see the sports spray," I say, holding out my hand.

The big hairy monster gives in to me. He slips his hand into his pocket, and when he brings it out his thick fingers are wrapped around a small pump spray container, and he drops it in my palm.

I step outside the shed where the light is better and read the label. It's called Big Gorilla. No kidding. It's like a joke. I would wonder what sort of idiot could put this ridiculous name on their product, but obviously some people are buying it.

I take a notebook out of my backpack, and write Big Gorilla on the inside back page. Below the name I very carefully copy out the main ingredient, checking the spelling four times. It's something called 4-androsenediol.

I hand the spray back to Franco. "I'll look it up on the computer at home tonight."

"I already know what it is," says Franco. "It converts to testosterone. But I never thought that Taylor..."

He turns his back. Could he be crying?

Do I put my arm around him? I would only reach up to his waist, I don't know if that would provide him much comfort. Besides, can a shrimp comfort a gorilla? I suppose I could take his hand, but that's where the testosterone contamination comes from, the skin-to-skin contact, that's what happened to Taylor.

I consider this for a moment, then slip my tiny hand inside his great paw. I put my other hand on top of his, I sandwich his hand between my own and give it a really good rub.

I have remembered my solo hair.

This may be the only chance I'll get.

I'm thinking how clever I am, rubbing away on Franco's hand, when I catch a movement at the edge of my vision and wheel around to see that Logan is watching us from the open back door.

# chapter
## twenty-four

"What's up?" says Logan. "I heard Franco shouting."

Franco whips his hand away from mine. "Tell him nothing," he whispers.

Logan's eyes are on me as he hesitates at the top of the stairs, his face a mixture of hurt and confusion. I glance up at Franco who is back to looking his usual menacing self.

"Logan is my boyfriend," I tell Franco. "I don't keep secrets from him. Secrets are toxic and pathological." I can't believe I said that last bit. I'm turning into my mother.

Before Franco can respond, I add, "He's going to find out sooner or later. Do you want him to hear about it from me or do you want to tell him yourself?"

Franco says, "All right, I'll tell him. That way it won't get all screwed up."

Oh this I want to hear.

So we walk to school together, all three of us, with me in the middle. Logan won't hold hands with me at first, which is understandable. Franco explains everything.

"You're spraying me with testosterone every morning?" says Logan.

"Basically," says Franco.

"To stop me from turning gay," says Logan. He shakes his head in disbelief.

"Taylor's been getting it too," I say.

"Accidentally," clarifies Franco.

"You mustn't say anything to anyone," I tell Logan. "Not because it's a secret though. Because it's private."

Logan takes my hand finally. "Right. It's a family issue," he says.

I'm not so sure about being family with the Losinos—all sorts of problems leap into my head, not the least being incest if Logan's and my relationship continues to develop. Logan squeezes my hand, and I understand that he isn't suggesting I join the family as his sister. I remember my mom saying that families came in all sorts of strange arrangements, so I decide to let go my worries on the matter and focus instead on our problem, which is Taylor.

"We need to find out if there's an antidote," I say.

"For testosterone?" says Logan.

"Yes," I say. "I could talk to Dr. Cleveland when she comes to the barn. I can work up some sort of question about hormones related to Turner Syndrome so she won't suspect anything."

Franco says, "I could post a question on my bodybuilders' forum. Maybe this happened before to someone else."

"It happened to my grandpa's girlfriend Isobel. She was contaminated by his testosterone cream," I say.

"Could you ask her?" says Logan. "Or would she figure it out and tell?" He turns to Franco and says, "Is that spray stuff legal, Franco? Could you be in some sort of parole violation?"

"I'm not on parole!" says Franco.

"You know what I mean," says Logan. "Would you have to go back to boot camp?"

"No—it's not illegal," says Franco. "But they would kick me off the team at school if they found out. I would hate that. My life would be over."

At least now I see something Taylor and Franco truly have in common: their dramatics around their lives being over. Maybe their old lives could be over together, and they could start something fresh. I decide not to mention this. Franco would probably think I was suggesting some sort of suicide pact for the pair of them, which of course I am not.

"Let's not give up yet," Logan says.

"Right," I say. "Franco and I will do our research, and get back together to discuss it tomorrow morning."

Franco grunts, which I take to mean that he agrees with this plan.

I stop on the sidewalk. "We have a pact," I say. I turn so we're all in a little huddle, and I put out my hand, palm down, and they each put out one of theirs, then we each add a hand to the stack, and I'm only being partly devious about this, trying for a bit more Big Gorilla on my skin, but I don't get much time anyway, because between Logan and Franco, racing up the sidewalk, faces all aglow, are Amber and Topaz.

"Oh brother," I say.

"Hi Logan," says Amber, and then with her voice dropping an octave, "Oh hi Franco, it's nice to see you without Taylor for a change."

"Hey Bambi," says Franco.

I think about correcting him, but then I check his face. He knows.

"It's Amber," she says, smile fading. She knows too.

"And Topaz," pipes up Topaz, who hasn't figured it out yet.

"We're having a family meeting," says Franco.

Amber's face turns pink. She stomps past us. "Right," she says, "pygmy chimp and the big gorilla, together at last."

"She doesn't take rejection very well," says Logan, watching their departing backs.

"Who does?" I say, thinking at first of Franco. I also think about myself, and how hard rejection has been on me, and I look at Amber skittering along ahead of us, laughing with Topaz, covering up as though nothing is wrong. I don't want to be part of this. Finally I'm in a position where Amber won't try to torment me and I could pay her back for everything she's done to me, and it doesn't feel right. There has to be a better way.

# chapter
## twenty-five

Logan walks with me back to his place after school. Mostly we talk about Mr. Brumby who is being extra-grumpy. I suggest that Mr. Brumby's testosterone levels might be too low because he's going through andropause.

"So on the one hand high testosterone can make people difficult like Franco's been since using that stupid spray," says Logan.

"And low testosterone is bad too," I say.

"You have to have it just right," says Logan.

"I guess so," I say.

"Life is very difficult," says Logan.

I couldn't agree with him more.

I leave Logan at his house, then ride Pinky out to the stable, which is deserted, except for the horses. Kansas's truck is there, but she doesn't come out to see me. Bernadette must be with her, because she doesn't appear either. Some watch dog. Fortunately Spike is always on duty keeping the horses safe.

Of course Taylor isn't there because she's at home shaving, and Dr. Cleveland is working.

It's perfect really—me and the horses.

I visit each of them, then take Brooklyn to the ring and let him go. He follows me around like a puppy. He stands beside the mounting block and lets me get on even though he's not wearing a halter or saddle. We walk around and I practice relaxing. I sit squarely on my seat bones and lift my sternum and drop my shoulders, and I visualize calmness and tranquility.

And Brooklyn slows to a stop, folds his legs and lies down beneath me.

I lean forward and put my arms around his neck and hug him with all the strength I can muster.

When I arrive back home for dinner, Mom and Dad aren't there. Isobel is in the kitchen peeling carrots for dinner while Grandpa has a nap.

"We sent your parents on a little vacation together," says Isobel. "Your grandpa and I will stay with you for the week."

I'm very grateful she hasn't said anything about *baby*sitting.

"Not that you need much help, I'm sure," continues Isobel, "but it's nice to have company."

"I think it's good that Mom and Dad are having a vacation," I say. "They haven't been getting along as well as usual."

"They told us you hadn't noticed, but I knew that wouldn't be the case," says Isobel. "I think they'll be fine though. They had a misunderstanding. It happens in couples sometimes. Your mom was able to do some research on the computer. She found she'd somehow subscribed to an excellent online science magazine, and was able to read a number of up-to-date articles about andropause which she passed on to your father."

"Oh that would be the magazine I signed her up for, when I was doing research about were-apes," I say. "I've been sloppy before using the computer and leaving a trail on the history file; at least this time I'm not in trouble—this time I've actually done a good thing, even if it is by accident.

"Were-apes?" says Isobel. "I don't believe I've heard of them."

"Oh, they're imaginary creatures," I say dismissively. "But my research led me to *Ardipithecus*, which is what I thought I saw at the river before I found out about sasquatches."

Isobel nods as though we're having a perfectly normal conversation. Mom would have turned it into a teaching opportunity about overactive imaginations and the potential misuse of the Internet. I know perfectly well that there's nonsense on the Web. Why is it that Isobel has more confidence in my abilities than my own mother has?

I lean against the warm oven door. Isobel is roasting something. Mom never has time for roasting, except for on major holidays like Thanksgiving, which usually becomes pretty frantic, so I can't say it's something I generally look forward to.

The kitchen air smells rich and steamy. I draw a deep breath and savour it. Plus it's wonderful to be having a relaxed adult conversation. I hate to ruin it even though this may be the perfect opportunity to quiz Isobel about what happened when she was contaminated with Grandpa's testosterone cream. I'm not quite sure how to bring it up but then Isobel takes up where she left off earlier.

"I remember how difficult my life was before my first husband was diagnosed and then had treatment for his andropause," she says.

"Dad's been pretty moody," I say, "and he never used to be. Mostly if there was a problem he just wasn't really here. Well, he'd be here and not here at the same time, if you know what I mean."

Isobel nods. "My ex-daughter-in-law said the same thing about my son."

"I never even knew he had a bad temper before," I say.

"It must have been very difficult for your mother, as a therapist, giving advice when she thought her own marriage was unraveling."

Unraveling? This seems extreme. I'm stunned into silence.

"I expect this is why she's become depressed," says Isobel.

My mother is depressed?

And I didn't notice?

It's too much to consider, that both my parents have been so deeply unhappy.

I have to try to change the subject. "Isobel, there's something I'd like to ask you about—confidentially. It's not about me really, but one of my friends."

"Oh I already know what you're getting at," says Isobel. "Not that I've breathed a word to anyone. When is she due?"

"Due?" I say.

"Kansas, your friend, when is her baby due?"

Kansas is pregnant?

Of course Kansas is pregnant. Suddenly I see it. How could I have missed putting together all the signs? Isobel picked it up in about five seconds. Isobel is so smart, and I am so dense.

I will never be good at life.

"It's another friend," I say, "with a different problem. I think she has the same problem you did, she's been accidentally contaminated with testosterone."

"Oh dear," says Isobel.

"She needs to know if the effects will go away."

"The effects?" says Isobel.

"She has man hair."

"Oh dear," says Isobel. "Sylvia, I don't know the answer to that. Do you suppose we could check the Internet?"

She dries her hands on a towel, and we go to the family room where Grandpa is snoring in an easy chair.

Isobel is awesome on the computer. She types really fast, and knows how to use good keywords in her questions. Still, after fifteen minutes, we don't know the answer. Google has never let me down before.

"Maybe she'll have to ask her doctor," says Isobel.

"She won't do that," I say. "She says her life is over."

"Whose life is over?" says Grandpa, peering over our shoulders at an article on hirsutism in Wikipedia. "Wow, look at that woman," says Grandpa.

"She's very hairy," says Isobel.

"I can see that," says Grandpa. He sounds appreciative. He sounds like he doesn't find this disgusting at all.

"You don't think it's gross?" I ask.

"It's very interesting," says Grandpa. "Not gross at all."

"So men wouldn't find a woman disgusting if she grew man hair?" I say.

"Depends on the man, 1 suppose," says Grandpa.

Isobel says, "When people love each other, it seems to not matter what they look like. Sometimes others find our flaws attractive."

"Like Isobel's nose," says Grandpa.

I can't believe he'd embarrass her like that, and wonder if maybe his senile dementia is returning, but then Isobel laughs.

"That's right, Henry," she says. "All my life I've been ashamed of this pointy big nose of mine, then I meet Henry and he tells me it's the first thing that attracted him to me."

"It was a beacon of love," says Grandpa.

# chapter
## twenty-six

After dinner my parents call from Tofino where they're renting a cabin. They have to use the pay phone by the office because they left their cell phones at home. Intentionally, so they say. They want to stay a week, if it's okay with me and Grandpa and Isobel, which it is of course. After we hang up, I check Mom and Dad's bedroom and find Mom's phone recharging on their dresser but there's no sign of Dad's BlackBerry or his recharger. I guess it's not so important for people in the financial industry to model good self-care, but I hope Mom doesn't find out before they come home.

Then Mr. Losino phones. He wants to speak to my mom or dad, but settles for Grandpa, who passes the phone back to me, saying whatever I decide is fine, he's sure I'm old enough to make decisions for myself.

Mr. Losino wants to include my account of my sighting in a book he is writing about sasquatches! I ask him if anecdotal evidence is okay in a scientific book, because my mom isn't impressed with it, but he says he prefers to think of it as testimonial evidence, which takes the value of sightings like mine to a higher level altogether. So wow! I'm going to testify for a book! He also wants my help with illustrations, so when my parents have returned from their vacation he'd like me to come over and he'll make a few drawings according to my instructions, just like when police sketch artists draw likenesses of crime suspects. He suggests I make some rough drawings myself in the mean time, to keep my memory fresh, and also to make some written notes of what I saw. Plus I can make up a pseudonym for myself! Mr. Losino wants my true identity to be protected, because people who report sasquatch sightings are often not treated with respect, and he can handle it himself because he's used to it, but he wouldn't want me to have to go through what he's gone through. He says he's very grateful for my participation.

I feel like a person in a witness protection program, which in a way I am. Picking a pseudonym is easy-peasy. I want to be "Lucy D," short for Lucid Dreamer, because that's what I am.

Though I decide that until I meet with Mr. Losino, I don't want to have any lucid dreams about sasquatches, because I don't want to mix up any of the images from my dreams with the images from my memory. So that night I make myself dream about Brooklyn, which isn't difficult at all. We gallop cross-country and leap bigger fences than I've seen in my life.

It's great to have a night free of sasquatches, unicorns, and body hair.

I wake up feeling refreshed and in charge of my life.

Grandpa and Isobel are already in the kitchen when I get there. Isobel is trying to read the ingredients listed on the margarine container and Grandpa is hanging up the phone.

"Why do they make the print so small?" says Isobel. Her head is tilted back so she can look through the bottom part of her glasses.

"It's non-hydrogenated," I tell her. "Mom won't buy any other kind."

"That was Sally on the phone," says Grandpa. "Taylor still has a migraine and is staying home from school again. Sally wants us to check in on her today. We should go right after breakfast. We can drop you at school on our way, Pipsqueak."

"Okay," I say without enthusiasm. This won't be a good idea. It will mean I can't walk with Logan. Even more importantly, Taylor needs some time alone. If the test kit arrived yesterday, she'll want to courier the samples to the lab today. I'm fumbling for an excuse when Isobel comes to my rescue.

"They're not babies, Henry. If Taylor has a migraine, she needs peace and quiet more than she needs company. We could check on her later in the day. Unless Sylvia *wants* a ride to school?"

Isobel is amazing.

"No, thanks anyway," I say. "I could use the fresh air and exercise." I know this is lame. Isobel looks at me as though she knows it too, but Grandpa just nods his head.

"Fine," he says. "That'll give me some time to organize Tony's workbench. It's a disaster."

This is not a good idea either. Dad is very particular about his workbench. Isobel looks from Grandpa to me and back to Grandpa again. I know how Mom would handle a situation like this. There would be a massive lecture about respecting personal space and boundaries.

Isobel says, "I was hoping we could go for a walk around the harbour this morning, Henry."

"That's an excellent idea," I say. "And maybe after your walk, you could have lunch out."

"Fish and chips!" says Grandpa.

Isobel glances at the margarine container and I'm all ready with information about the health risks of eating deep-fried foods, which I've heard a million times from Mom, but Isobel raises a finger and stops me.

"If you like, Henry," she says.

Interesting. Very interesting.

After breakfast I ride Pinky to Logan's house. I'd been looking forward to our walk to school, and sharing research results with Logan and Franco. As I pedal along, I grow more uneasy. When it comes down to it, I'm not sure I can trust Franco to do the right thing for Taylor. He might not be the kind of guy who likes women who are covered with man hair.

If only I could be more like Isobel. She understands all sorts of people and then carries out complex plans that cover all the bases. It's as though she knows what she wants to have happen and then sets out to make it so. She doesn't just react emotionally like everyone else does in my family. And she moves so subtly that most people don't even notice. Take this morning for example. She knew my dad would be upset if Grandpa reorganized his workbench, and she knew Grandpa wouldn't take kindly to being told so. The best way to solve the problem was to find something else for Grandpa to do, even if it meant compromising on their low-fat diet.

Maybe I can be crafty and flexible when I'm old like Isobel. But right now even though I know what I want to happen, a plan for how to get there is beyond me.

What I want is for Taylor to go back to being normal, and I can't do anything about that. She's either contaminated with testosterone or she isn't. If she is, only time will tell if the effects disappear or whether she's stuck with them for life.

The outcome is totally out of my hands.

It's weird, because only an hour ago I woke up from my

dreams and felt strong and in charge of my life, and already I am smacked up against my limitations. I'm happy that I've stopped feeling like a helpless kid, but it seems to me that even as a crafty planner there's only so much you can do. Life is very strange.

Logan is waiting for me when I get to his house, but he's on his own.

"Where's Franco?" I say.

"He said his coach told him he had to go in early for practice," says Logan.

"You don't believe him?"

"He didn't say anything about it yesterday," says Logan.

"At least he's showing some responsibility for his team," I say.

"You're taking his side?"

I guess Logan is still feeling sensitive about catching me holding Franco's hand yesterday. I can't tell him why I did it. Instead I take his hand. "It's better with just you and me anyway," I say. "There's probably nothing we can do, other than support each other."

"And Taylor," says Logan.

"Right. Taylor's the one with the major personal crisis. She's going to need lots of support."

"We can do that," says Logan. For once he doesn't finish up with a joke. As much as I've always appreciated how Logan is a jokester, I'm surprised to realize I can like him even more when he isn't.

# chapter
## twenty-seven

After an uninspiring day at school, I bike to the barn. Kansas isn't there, but I'm hoping she'll show up by the time I've changed and tacked up Brooklyn, because I really really want a lesson today. I need to take my mind off life for a while. I hope Kansas is okay. I wonder if she's happy about being pregnant. I don't think it was in her plans, though she has been showing signs of being broody lately, adopting Bernadette and even talking about getting a cat next, of all things. I don't know any cats personally. I was scratched by one once, when I was five. I was trying to rescue a kitten from where Bunga had chased it under some bushes. The cat didn't make a good impression on me, given that I was trying to help and it attacked me. I'm not sure that cats are trustworthy. So based on my experience, given a choice between a cat and a baby, it's better that Kansas is pregnant. Unless she delivers a baby like Erika. Or twins. Twins would be really bad.

I'm unlatching Brooklyn's stall door when I hear a truck drive into the yard. I'm all excited about seeing Kansas, but when I reach the door at the end of the alleyway, I see that it's Declan.

He notices the disappointment on my face. "What's up?" he says.

I sigh. "I wanted a jumping lesson. But Kansas isn't here."

"I could teach you," says Declan.

"You? I didn't know you rode."

"I used to ride. It's still all up here," he says, tapping his forehead with a finger. "I'll set up a grid for you. How high have you been jumping?"

Well, that's an interesting question. Kansas is so cautious that we've hardly been jumping more than a foot high. But in my dreams, that's another matter. I turn to Brooklyn beside me, my trusty trusting steed. What would he like to do? "Three feet," I say.

Declan hesitates. "You don't say." He strokes Brooklyn's neck. "How about we start you two with something smaller, then see how you deal with more height."

All right. This is going to be fantastic.

Out at the ring, I buckle on my helmet, lead Brooklyn to the mounting block, and climb aboard. While Declan sets up the jumps, I have to warm up our muscles.

Brooklyn is in a very good mood, I can tell by how he starts right away with a long swinging walk, and I can feel he wants to trot. I'm not ready yet though. First I have to go through the checklist Kansas taught me: feet equally weighted in stirrups of equal length; equal weight on seat bones; shoulders open and relaxed; arms and elbows relaxed; neck tall and collarbones lifted. Check check check.

"What are you thinking about?" says Declan.

"I'm making sure I'm straight and in balance," I say.

"I see," says Declan.

"Because if I'm not straight and balanced, the horse can't be straight and balanced," I say, quoting Kansas. Though why

I should have to explain this to Declan, I don't understand. Maybe he doesn't know as much about riding as he thinks he does. I hope this doesn't turn into a mess.

"What's your favourite song?" says Declan.

I am picking up my reins, making sure they are firmly and evenly held between fingers, thumbs and palms. I have to remind myself to relax my arm and lower my shoulders again. I'm too busy concentrating on riding correctly so even if I wanted to I couldn't answer Declan's silly question.

"I don't sing," I say.

"Everyone sings," says Declan. "It makes whatever you're doing more fun, and gets you out of your head."

"You need to talk to my mom," I say, laughing.

"There, that's better," says Declan. "Your horse is more relaxed now, he likes it when you laugh. Twice around the arena now at the trot, and you better be singing."

So I sing that silly *Hills-are-alive* song, which makes me wonder if the sasquatch is watching us from the woods, and how ridiculous we would look in his eyes, running around in circles, which makes me laugh again.

Brooklyn is going like a little steam train.

"Great," says Declan. "Now come up the quarter line and trot through the grid."

"Ground poles?" I say. "I thought we were going to jump."

"Quarter line," says Declan. So I see he is going to be no pushover.

Still, it's exciting. We're starting our jumping lesson! I aim Brooklyn toward the trotting poles and he charges through them.

Declan calls me into the center of the ring. He strokes Brooklyn's neck. "There is a difference," he says, "between riding a horse and being a passenger. Your job is to guide

Brooklyn until he knows what to do. You set the speed as well as direction. It's not just point and shoot, no matter how perfect your position may be."

I nod. I think I get it.

"Try the grid again, set the pace before you get there, and then maintain it. You may not have to do much more than think it, your horse can pick it up from you."

"You mean psychically?" I say.

"Not exactly," says Declan. "Try it anyway."

I trot a couple of circles at the end of the arena, fixing our rhythm in my mind, then turn my head in the direction of the poles. Brooklyn trots through them as though they aren't even there.

"Brilliant," says Declan.

He sets up two jumps on the other long side of the arena. They're maybe a foot high. "Four strides between them," says Declan.

"What?" I say.

"Has Kansas not told you this? You need to help Brooklyn approach the jumps properly and take off at the right point, so you have to be able to lengthen and shorten his stride."

"Right. I must have forgotten." I don't want him to see how much of a beginner I am, or he'll keep the jumps down at baby height.

We do the jumps perfectly, first time, four strides.

"Hmmm," says Declan. "Now do it again, three strides this time."

I circle at the end of the arena, visualizing three strides. I'll need more push, but not too much, or Brooklyn will flatten. He won't be able to stand off too much from the first fence, we'll have to hit that one just right. I turn my head to the jump and Brooklyn turns too. He takes the first fence perfectly, then I sit and push him for the second.

"Amazing," says Declan.

I don't dare tell him that I practice at night in my dreams. I don't know that Declan will understand. I hardly understand myself, but this must be the only explanation, because I haven't been practicing this sort of thing with Kansas.

Declan sets up another jump on the diagonal. Two poles, one above the other.

"Now, when you're lining up for this one, I want you to pick your take-off spot when you come out of the corner, and count aloud your strides into the jump. Like this." Declan demonstrates, walking around the corner, taking long exaggerated strides, counting four-three-two-one, and ending up at the perfect spot before the jump.

My first time around the corner, I start counting at ten, and am at the take-off spot when I say six.

"Good work," says Declan. "Try again." He's standing beside the jump. When I canter down the long side, in my peripheral vision, I can see he raises the top pole. I don't have time to see how much it's raised, because I have to pick my line, and my take-off spot, and count the strides.

It takes two more tries before I get it right and then Declan tells me to give Brooklyn a rest.

"You two are naturals," he says.

Brooklyn and I are both breathing hard. It's more work than in my dreams, but I don't care. I was born for this. It's the most exciting thing I've done in my whole life. It's like flying, only better.

"Of course, you've jumped three feet before," says Declan.

I look at the jump. I was so busy concentrating on other things that I hadn't noticed. It's huge. "That's three feet?"

"We won't tell Kansas though, will we?" Declan removes

the top pole and lays it on the ground. "No sense exciting the woman unnecessarily."

I jumped three feet! And I'm not dreaming!

"Thank you, Declan," I say.

"It was my pleasure. You and that pony are remarkably attuned to one another."

I consider this. I thought everyone was attuned to their horse like I was to Brooklyn. But maybe not. "I can make him lie down," I say. I'm not sure this is a good thing, and probably Kansas wouldn't approve, she'd think it was dangerous, but Declan has a different attitude.

"As a trick?" says Declan.

"I don't think so," I say. "It's more a matter of communication."

Declan raises his eyebrows. "Show me," he says.

So I give Brooklyn a teensy squeeze with my legs and guide him to the middle of the ring, all the while relaxing and relaxing and stilling my mind. Brooklyn slows, and stops, and folds gently to the ground.

"Now I've seen everything," says Declan.

# chapter
## twenty-eight

I never thought I'd say this, but by Wednesday morning I'm missing my mom and dad.

Grandpa and Isobel are really nice, and maybe that's the problem, maybe they're too nice instead of being family. Being with them all the time is like eating too much chocolate.

It's great to tell them about my jumping lesson, but it's as though they get excited for me without really appreciating how significant it was. They would have acted just as excited if I said I'd jumped a one-foot cross-pole. My parents would have known how big a deal it really was for me. Of course they might not have liked it very much, being even bigger safety-freaks than Kansas. Still, I would have liked to be able to tell them.

Something else I thought I'd never say is that I found a riding instructor I like better than Kansas. I had so much fun riding with Declan, and I can't see that happening again. My parents would never go for it, he's not certified, probably doesn't carry any insurance, and worse still I couldn't betray Kansas this way.

I struggle with myself all morning, trying not to feel sad, though I probably don't do a great job of it because

Logan tells me even more jokes than usual and I have to make myself laugh at them so his feelings don't get hurt.

Then something deeply disturbing happens at school.

I'm taking my usual route to math class, avoiding the main hallway where it's too easy for me to get trampled, and in the stairwell outside the furnace room, I come upon Franco necking with Amber. Amber has her back to me, but I know right away it's her because her signature black bra straps show outside the edges of her sleeveless blouse. Franco looks up mid-pucker and sees me. He isn't embarrassed. He considers me calmly. I feel like it's the first time he's seen me as a real person. It's as though he's acknowledging me, as though he and I have an understanding, as though he knows me and can count on me to not rat him out to Taylor. I feel strangely flattered and important and at the same time I am completely disgusted with myself.

This all happens over no more than five seconds, then Franco returns to where he left off and I scurry away before Amber notices.

I'm all churned up and can't concentrate during math class so of course Mr. Brumby yells at me and probably would have given me a detention if Logan hadn't drawn his fire by putting up his hand and asking a question. Logan has no problems with math, he doesn't need to ask questions. I know he did this to rescue me. He's so kind and good, it's hard to understand how he could be related to Franco, unless maybe Franco was adopted…or the product of an unfortunate relationship when Mrs. Losino was young and before she met Mr. Losino. Young and foolish like Taylor, who picked the completely wrong boyfriend for herself. I've known this all along in my bones, but didn't have the hard evidence until today. Now I don't know what to do about it. If I tell Taylor, she'll be hurt, and Franco will hate me. If

I don't tell her, bad-boy Franco will respect me, but Taylor won't know that Franco is a cheat, and she might go back to him.

On the other hand, maybe it was a set-up and Franco *wants* me to tell Taylor, to make her jealous and take him back. In which case I shouldn't tell her.

Tell. Don't tell. When in doubt, forward. When in doubt, don't.

What a mess.

One thing I do know: Amber and Franco are made for each other.

I feel like an orphan with no one to talk to. Taylor is still hiding behind her migraine. I can't talk to Logan, because Franco is his brother. My mom and dad are away on vacation. Kansas is AWOL. And everything seems much too complicated to explain to Isobel and Grandpa.

At the barn Wednesday afternoon, I can't bring myself to ride. I'm afraid of what emotions I might accidentally communicate to Brooklyn. I hang out with him in his paddock, pick the tangles out of his tail with my fingers, and give him three whole apples from the feed room even though Kansas says I'm never to give him more than two because of the risk of him developing insulin resistance. He nuzzles me when he's finished, and since his lips are covered with applesauce, pretty soon I'm covered with applesauce too, and I don't know why, but this makes me laugh. I let him lick my fingers, and he's very careful and I never feel a tooth, so I know he'd never bite me. He's my best friend. And I don't have to tell him a thing.

Which is different from my situation with Taylor.

Tell. Don't tell. Go forward. Don't.

That evening, Taylor comes out of seclusion and phones

me. I've been getting updates on her condition from Grandpa and Isobel, who visit her every day and report back to me over dinner. They're worried because Taylor is still saying she has a migraine.

"I sent away my saliva samples," she says. "How long do you think they will take to get back to me?"

"How should I know?" I say.

"The package went overnight express," she says.

"Maybe tomorrow then," I say.

"I miss Franco," says Taylor.

Great. Next she's going to ask me if I've seen him, and I don't know if I can convince her with a lie. For some reason, I remember Declan telling me not to be a passenger. I can do something. I can offer some guidance. "Everyone's worried about you," I say. "Grandpa and Isobel think you have a brain tumor."

"Hmmph," says Taylor.

"It's not fair to worry your family. You can't stay home forever."

She hangs up on me.

I guess I should have said something else. Maybe I should have sung to her.

# chapter
## twenty-nine

I'm not very good at waiting, but it seems that's all I can do. Wait for my parents to come home on Saturday. Wait for Taylor's test results. Wait for Kansas to feel better. Wait for Mr. Losino to interview me about my sasquatch sightings.

Thursday is pretty uneventful, except for lunchtime. I'm sitting at a table, by myself because Logan has chess club, and Franco saunters by. He stops, looks at me, and winks.

He is so sure I'm on his side it makes me sick.

What makes it worse is that, as he turns to leave, I catch a whiff of liniment. He's still using the stuff. He doesn't care about anyone but himself.

Mr. Losino picks up Logan from school because they have to do some shopping in town so I have to walk by myself. At least I hope I'll be by myself, and that I won't be joined by my tormentors. I wait an extra fifteen minutes inside the school building to give Amber and Topaz time to clear out, then I take an indirect route through the neighbourhood to make sure I avoid them. Eventually I retrieve Pinky from the Losinos' shed, but by then it's pouring with rain so there's no point in going to the barn. After dinner, Grandpa and Isobel make me play Scrabble with them and given my difficulties with spelling, this is no fun at all.

To bring my spirits up, that night I try to dream about Brooklyn. I do manage to ride him, but I'm sitting on his back and I'm holding a Scrabble board on my lap. Every time Brooklyn takes a step, the tiles slide all over the place. Someone is telling me to read the words. Read the words! Read the words! Okay, okay, I'm trying! Eventually the tiles line up, but it's only four letters, and I'm thinking they won't be worth much even on a double word square, but then I see what they spell: T-E-L-L.

This doesn't do anything to raise my spirits. In fact it has the opposite effect, so when I wake up Friday morning all I can think about is that this is the day I will ruin Taylor's life. Again.

It doesn't help that Logan is weirdly happy on the walk to school. I don't want to ruin his mood, but also don't want to fake that everything's okay, because I wouldn't want him to fake it with me if the situation was reversed. I tell him I'm not happy at all, and that I have to give Taylor some bad news.

Logan squeezes my hand. "You're a good friend," he says. "You'll do the right thing. Who knows, maybe something will happen today to cheer you up."

I'm surprised that he doesn't ask me what the bad news is, and I'm trying to deal with that when he giggles, which strikes me as totally inappropriate and stuns me into silence. We walk half a block and I still can't figure out what to say. Logan starts humming, and I decide to let it go. I have enough to deal with without adding more drama. I hum along with him to show there's no bad feelings, which there aren't really. It's just my usual confusion.

The school day drags on and on, even though I'm

dreading the end of the day when I have to tell Taylor what Franco's been up to. Maybe I'll phone her after dinner. Or maybe I could send her an email—that would be the easiest thing for me, and the best thing for Taylor because it would give her the privacy to digest the news. I think about how upset she will be, on top of how upset she already is about the man hair she's growing. Maybe it isn't fair. Maybe she doesn't need to know, and I should let things sort out on their own. Why add to her troubles just because I had a dream?

So I change my mind. I won't tell her. I'll get on with my own business. I'll meet Logan after school, walk to his place, grab Pinky, and then go see Brooklyn. Maybe I'll even take Brooklyn on a trail ride. Maybe I'll go sasquatch hunting. I have a plan and I'll stick to it.

It's like I'm counting my strides to my take-off point, but life isn't going to let me get there.

First, there's a problem with Logan. He's goofing around during afternoon phys ed class, running backwards and dribbling the basketball, trying to make me laugh again. He trips, falls and hurts his wrist. He insists it's fine, but Mr. Rouncy says his scaphoid bone could be cracked, which would be very serious apparently, so Mrs. Losino has to pick up Logan and take him to Emergency for an x-ray. Logan turns to look at me as he's led out of the gymnasium, and his wrist must hurt more than he was letting on, because his face is agonized.

I have to walk to his house to collect Pinky on my own. Okay, I've done this before, I can do it again. Today I'm not wasting time like I did yesterday. I slip out a side door and take the direct route, mostly at a run.

I'm breathing heavily by the time I reach the Losinos' garden shed, and that's when I get the shock of my life.

I slide open the door and see that Pinky has been transformed.

My bike now looks like something exotic that Avril Lavigne would ride.

The handgrips are black, the seat is black, so are the pedals. There are two new black fenders and a black rear carrier rack. Four black neoprene skins have been fitted over the frame. The dreadful expanse of pink has been reduced considerably. Over the handlebar is draped the coolest pair of curved black-rimmed protective eyeglasses. I pick them up. The arms are flexible. I can adjust them so the glasses sit perfectly in front of my eyes despite my ears being lower than most normal people's.

Now this is a bike I could take to school, except that now it's so cool looking I don't know how long before it would be stolen, despite the new black cable and padlock with keys.

Plus there's a bigger problem.

Franco was the one who suggested I get rid of the white seat and handgrips. Franco is responsible. Obviously he is trying to buy my silence.

I am so deeply offended that I can hardly breathe. I feel like there's a brick on my chest, and I know it's not going to go away until I do the right thing.

So instead of biking to the barn, I turn in the direction of Taylor's house. This is an hour ride, but some things have to be done immediately, face-to-face, not by e-mail or phone. I'm so determined it's as though I'm full of jet fuel, and my legs pump the pedals with an energy I've never felt before.

Any time my legs weaken in the slightest, I think about how Franco has betrayed by dear cousin. I recall his face when I caught him with Amber, full of smug confidence. I think about him winking at me in the cafeteria. I am ashamed and disgusted at how close I came to selling out. I have seen a dark side of myself that I didn't know existed.

I also find myself locked in a hopeless battle over whether I love or hate my transformed Pinky.

I arrive at Taylor's house physically and emotionally exhausted. Auntie Sally isn't home, and no one is answering the front door. I check the handle, but it's locked.

I know Taylor's in there.

Bunga is in the backyard barking his head off as usual. I unlatch the side gate and shove Bunga away when he launches himself at my knee. I try the kitchen door, and it's locked too. I can see the glow of the computer screen through Taylor's window. I have to talk to her.

Bunga disappears between my legs through the dog door. He stands in the kitchen and barks at me some more. Such an annoying little dog, not at all intelligent or respectable like Bernadette.

Then out of nowhere I understand what he's trying to tell me, as though I am a hearing-impaired animal communicator, a little slow to pick up on the psychic message. I push at the dog door with my hand so it flaps in, then out, and slaps shut again. The door was installed by a previous resident, for a larger dog than Bunga. I kneel in front of it. A normal human being couldn't manage, but it seems there are at times advantages to being a pygmy. I have to turn my shoulders sideways, but at least I don't have any wide hips to worry about, and in seconds I'm lying inside on the kitchen floor, trying to stop Bunga from sticking his tongue in my ear.

I knock at Taylor's door. She doesn't answer, and I walk in anyway, closing the door behind me so Bunga doesn't bug us.

Taylor looks awful. She hasn't combed her hair. She's

still wearing her pajamas, powder blue cotton flannel with puffy white clouds and angels and golden falling stars, buttoned snugly to the neck. She's resting her head on one hand propped by its elbow on the arm of her chair.

Wordlessly she points to the screen of the computer, then swivels her chair and slouches off to sit on her bed.

I check the screen. Taylor has received her test results via e-mail. It's a disaster.

# chapter
## thirty

Taylor is loaded with testosterone. The bio-lab says the only way a girl can have levels this high is if she's taking testosterone supplements or she's been contaminated by an external source.

"Franco," I say.

"I know," says Taylor. "He didn't mean to, I really shouldn't judge him, he was just…"

"Dumb," I say.

Taylor nods.

"And self-centered and uncaring," I say. I try to use a gentle objective tone. I try to filter out the anger I feel for Franco, but it must leak anyway.

Taylor glares at me. There are dark circles under her eyes, she hasn't brushed her teeth, and her eyebrows look like they've been run over by a lawn mower—I guess these hairs have been growing too, and she has attempted a trim. Despite her exhaustion, she still she has the energy to defend Franco. "You don't know him like I do," she says. "He phoned last night and told me how important I am to him, and it's totally fine if I have a bit more body hair than I used to—he says I'll look more like an Italian."

"An Italian?" I say. I can't believe she's bought this load of nonsense.

"He's not what he seems, Sylvia. He hasn't had an easy life. You of all people should know not to judge someone by his appearance."

Because this hurts me, and because I'm so exhausted, I tell her point-blank that on Wednesday I saw Franco necking with Amber in the stairwell at school.

Taylor collapses onto her bed. She covers her face with her hands and wails.

"You're sure?" she says between sobs.

I tell her yes.

"I don't know why I'm so upset," she says. "We were through anyway, I could never forgive him for what he's done to me." She cries some more, but I don't know if it's over losing Franco or because of her test results, and maybe Taylor doesn't know either.

I sit down beside her, and tell her the other part, about Franco trying to buy my silence by refitting Pinky, and how I hated Pinky being so pink before, and I like all the black accessories now, but maybe I should tear them off because this just isn't right, and then I'm crying too.

On the other side of the bedroom door, Bunga howls, a pathetic scratchy bugle, as though he's never tried this before in his life. Taylor sniffs. "That's worse than Spike's braying," she says, which was exactly what I was thinking but of course I couldn't say so.

Taylor sits up, reaches for the tissue box on her bedside table and plunks it between us. She blows her nose, runs her fingers through her hair then looks at me, frowning deeply.

"You call your bike *Pinky*?" she says. And unbelievably, in the midst of her personal tragedy, she laughs, and has to blow her nose again, and then I laugh and cry at the same time and we go through about a hundred tissues until we're more or less back to normal.

Taylor runs her fingers across her upper lip. "Do you see my mustache?" she asks.

I blink hard to remove the last of my tears, and lean closer and examine the short fuzzy growth. "Logan's is definitely a lot thicker," I say, thinking this should make her feel better.

She's not pleased. "Oh great," she says.

"Maybe it will go away now you've stopped getting the testosterone," I say.

"I'll probably have to go for laser hair removal," says Taylor. She shudders. "Everywhere," she adds.

"My mom has a gift certificate that she's not going to use until hell freezes over," I say.

Taylor sighs heavily.

"You could go to your doctor," I say. "Maybe he can tell you if you have to do something or just wait for it to go away."

"Are you kidding? Mom still takes us to Dr. Destrie. He'd take one look at me and have a heart attack. I've been doing research on the Internet and there's nothing about how permanent this hair is. Dr. Destrie's so ancient and out of date he wouldn't have a clue."

I don't tell her that Isobel and I couldn't find anything in our research either, but I am reminded of Grandpa's reaction to the woman with hirsutism. "Taylor, maybe some men like hairy women," I say. "Not just Italian men, I mean."

She shakes her head as though this isn't remotely possible.

I try again. "Sometimes people love us *because* of our flaws," I say.

"Not Franco apparently," she says.

"Spike still loves you," I say.

"I've been neglecting Spike," says Taylor. "I haven't wanted to go to the barn, I didn't want anyone to see me." She slides off the bed, shuffles to her desk and picks up the framed photograph of Spike. She kisses her finger and presses it to the glass on top of his nose. "Sorry, Spike," she says. She's silent for a moment, studying the picture. Then she turns to me, alarmed. "Spike says *stinky dog*. That's all he says, over and over, like that other time. What's going on?"

Without thinking about how Taylor is scared of everything, and really doesn't need more trouble right now, I jump to my feet and blurt out, "The sasquatch is back!"

Taylor's eyes go wide, and a hand flutters to her throat and then, against all my expectations, she says, "I love sasquatches!"

My wonderful magical cousin. I had no idea. She stands there with Spike's picture held tight to her apparently hairy chest, her face suddenly alive with possibilities.

"Have you seen one?" she says.

"I saw two," I tell her. "A male and a female."

She doesn't ask me if I'm sure, she doesn't suggest I saw bears, or people pulling pranks. "I always knew they were real," she says. "Franco freaked when I mentioned it one day, he said I was an idiot. He never supported me, not really."

I figure she might as well know the whole truth, so I tell her that Franco's dad isn't a computer expert as Franco told her, he's a wildlife biologist who's writing a book about sasquatches.

Taylor shakes her head in amazement. "He was such a liar. I should have known better. Well, I did know better, part of me always knew he wasn't right for me, but another part…" She reaches for Franco's picture and drops it in her waste basket, adjusting it so the face is down. "Does Mr. Losino know what you saw?"

"Oh yes, Logan told him," I say. "He's including my sightings in a book he's writing. He says I've discovered something very important to science."

"Wow," says Taylor. "Do you think you could show them to me?"

"Sure. We could go on a search party, you and me and Brooklyn and Spike. Mr. Losino says the best way to see sasquatches is from horseback." But I'm thinking, What about Logan? I know he'll want to come too, but if I invite him, he'll bring his bike, and his being there will change things between me and Taylor.

It doesn't seem fair that I have to choose, but I do.

"I should tell Spike about the sasquatch," says Taylor. She gazes at his photo. "He needs to know it's not a smelly dog." She closes her eyes and the message wafts off through space. I wish I could say that I saw sparks fly out of her head, or watched her aura change, but I can't. I suppose I'm too much a scientist. I want to believe, but deep down, I don't. Not that I need to tell this to Taylor.

Bunga has stopped howling, and is instead scratching furiously at the closed door and making his usual yipping noises. Taylor replaces Spike's photo on her desk and opens the door, I think to let Bunga join us, but instead she stands in the hallway and motions for me to follow. "Show me what's happened to Pinky," she says.

I take her outside to where Pinky is leaning against the house beside the front door.

Taylor is impressed. "Very cool bike," she says.

I point out all the new modifications and she examines them carefully.

"You know, Sylvia, Franco wouldn't have done something like this. Even if he'd thought of it, he couldn't have done this good a job. Someone's been very careful and creative here."

For a second I think that Logan has done it, and my heart speeds up as I imagine him toiling over my bike renovations, and I wonder how I could ever repay him or show him my appreciation, and then Taylor says, "It must have been Mr. Losino, in gratitude for the information for his book."

Of course she's right. Logan was in school all day, he wouldn't have had the time and, unlike Franco, he wouldn't skip out. Though probably he knew what his dad was going to do, probably he wanted to be there with me when I found my bike, but instead he had to get his hand x-rayed, and that was why he looked so upset when he left the gym.

"Oh that's great," I say.

It is great—because I can enjoy my new bike (which I will rename Avril Lavigne) and I won't have to feel disloyal to Taylor or that I'm owing anything to Franco. I also don't mind that I don't owe anything to Logan. Relationships with boys are complicated.

"I think I'll be single for a while," says Taylor. "I'll need some time for my heart to heal."

"You won't be lonely?" I say.

Taylor shrugs. "Probably. There are worse things."

"You could have been pregnant," I say.

"Like Kansas," says Taylor. When she sees the surprise on my face, she explains, "Spike told me he thought she was in foal. He says Kansas is very excited but needs to keep it secret for a while."

I nod in mute agreement. I am so relieved that Kansas is happy about the turn her life has taken, that I cannot speak.

We stand shoulder to shoulder, considering Avril Lavigne, and life.

Taylor will be fine on her own for a while, with time to find her direction in life and develop her talents unhindered.

I realize that the same applies to me. For starters, I can enjoy designing a scientific experiment to determine whether my cousin really is psychic or whether, like Isobel, she is eerily perceptive.

Besides, until Taylor has the laser hair removal, she's going to have a difficult time at school. It will be hard for her, someone who's always been pretty and popular, especially if Amber develops a campaign, and why wouldn't she?

Fortunately, Taylor has someone to show her the ropes, someone who's been in leper-land before her. Taylor has me.

Taylor sighs. "I wish I could stop feeling like a victim."

"You could report Franco to his coach," I say tentatively. "He'd get kicked off the team."

Her face brightens but only momentarily. "I couldn't do that. He lives for sports."

"Not just sports," I say, still feeling the need for some revenge. "There's also Amber."

Taylor slowly shakes her head. "Amber doesn't have a clue what she's getting into. If we don't do something, she'll be contaminated too."

Even I don't dislike Amber enough to want this to happen.

"It's not a kindness to Franco to let him continue either," says Taylor. "It's unhealthy to take steroids, he'll end up needing organ transplants. We have to do something."

"Franco doesn't listen to anybody," I say. "Not his parents, not his brother."

"He used to listen to me sometimes," says Taylor. "Maybe he'll listen to Amber."

"I could have a word with Topaz," I say.

"Maybe if we all work together," says Taylor.

"Like a herd."

"Speaking of which," says Taylor, plucking at her pajamas,

"my herd is due back any minute now—Mom's bringing Erika home from swim class. I need to return to my cave."

"I bet if we phoned Grandpa and Isobel, they'd pick us up and take us to the barn. You could see Spike."

Taylor shakes her head. "Not today. I'm not quite ready. I'd like some more time on my own to absorb…everything."

"I understand," I say, but I'm disappointed. Going to the barn would be a great first step. She can't stay in her room forever,

"How about tomorrow?" says Taylor. "Mom's taking Erika to a swim meet. I can sneak out without being interrogated."

Thank goodness. It's not school, but it's a start. "Great idea," I say.

"I'll wear my hat, and gloves. Grandpa and Isobel won't notice anything," says Taylor.

Ha! Isobel notices everything. I catch myself just before saying so out loud.

# chapter
## thirty-one

I think Taylor looks odd wearing her hat and gloves in the car, but no one says anything. Grandpa and Isobel drop us at the stable, then head off to watch the swim meet for a while.

Kansas is around back leaning on the fence of the isolation paddock. Bernadette is leashed and sitting at her feet. They're watching a horse I don't recognize, a sorrel, head down, picking nonchalantly at a pile of hay.

"Who's that?" I ask.

"We have a new boarder," says Kansas.

I like how she says *we*. My chest feels cramped, in a nice way, as if it needs more room to hold my heart.

"She's a barrel racer," Kansas continues. "Her name's Dudette."

Taylor and I exchange a glance. *Dudette*. Would that be a male dude with female features? Or a female with male characteristics? I shrug. What does it really matter?

"The family just moved out from Ponoka. I haven't worked with a barrel horse for donkey's ears," Kansas muses, then apologizes to Taylor.

"No problem," says Taylor. She loves Spike's ears, while

Kansas has never had any success at hiding her scorn for the long pointy things.

"Are you going to be teaching her dressage, Kansas?" I say, because this is her passion, or at least it was before Declan and the foal-to-be came along.

"Not exactly, though the same principles of flexion and bending and collection apply. Terminology is different. I won't be talking about half-halts. We'll work on rating and whoa spots instead."

"It's all about the bond anyway," says Taylor. "No matter what discipline you follow, it all comes down to the relationship you have with your horse."

Kansas clears her throat. "Horses aren't poodles. They can kill you without meaning to. They need discipline and training more than bonding."

"Spike wouldn't kill me," says Taylor. "He only ever bites me as a show of affection."

"Don't come running to me when he affectionately takes your ear off," says Kansas.

Taylor snorts.

They're never going to agree, and I don't care. I can see where they're coming from and I can love them both. There's no need to jump in the middle. Isobel would be proud of me.

A happy sigh escapes my lungs. It's so great that everything's getting back to normal.

An old Mazda pickup lurches into sight on the driveway and rattles towards the parking area.

"Who's that?" says Taylor.

"Must be Dudette's owner," says Kansas. "She told me her brother was going to drop her off this morning."

I feel Taylor stiffen beside me. She's not ready for new people. She ducks in behind Kansas because there's no point trying to duck in behind me.

The truck stops beside the barn and the doors groan open. A teenage girl springs from the passenger side, looking around wildly until her eyes fall upon Dudette. It's as if she's been hit by a magical freezing spell. She stands and stares. She doesn't move a muscle until Dudette raises her head and nickers softly in her direction.

Ah. Good Person. No label required.

I'm less sure about the brother. Tall and sinewy, dressed in black jeans and T-shirt, he has unfolded his long limbs and arisen from the driver side. His arms are tattooed in shades of blue all the way down to his wrists so it looks like he's wearing sleeves but he's not. Weird. Why would anyone do this?

"Keep your hands off that boy now, Sylvia," Kansas teases me.

I'm about to say, "No problem there," when Taylor almost dislocates my shoulder as she charges past me, whispering fiercely, "Don't you touch him, he's mine."

Yup. All back to normal, I'd say.

# Acknowledgments

I would not be able to pursue my passions of writing and riding without the support and encouragement of a community of people, at the core of which are my family and friends.

Thank you to Randal Macnair and Christa Moffat at Oolichan Books, and to my wonderful editor, Alison Acheson. What a pleasure it is to work with nice people.

I am very grateful to the young women with Turner Syndrome and their families, for sharing with me, either directly or so candidly on their blogs and YouTube.

For information about the sasquatch I am indebted to *The Discovery of the Sasquatch: Reconciling Culture, History, and Science in the Discovery Process* by John A. Bindernagel. 2010. Beachcomber Books, Courtenay, British Columbia.

Thank you to the readers of early drafts: Anna Elvidge, Seiko Marton and Kim McCarley.

There are many people who have assisted me over the years in my adventures with horsemanship. Thanks to Dave Bowron and Pat Bowron for starting me off, and finding that essential first great horse for me. Thanks to Norah Ross for honing my jumping skills. Thanks to Ralph Mortimer for showing me there's a whole other way to ride. Thanks to Gina Allen for keeping me straight in the saddle. Thanks to Alexi Buffalo for help with the barrel horse. Thanks to Pam Asheton for reminding me of some magic.

Thanks to Michael Collins at The Broken Spoke Bicycle Shop for strategies on transforming Pinky.

Thanks to Isobel Springett for another wonderful cover photo, and to Baylee Kivela and her pony, Elodon McCrae, for being such willing and truly perfect participants in the photoshoot.

Thank you, Cassie Hobenshield, for allowing me to borrow Dudette.

Thanks to Lollipop and Huckles, for ensuring I get my butt out of my garret and down to the barn.

Thank you, Shadow. (He knows why.)

And Mike, thank you for tolerating the clutter, for bringing me coffee just the way I like it, listening carefully to draft after draft, and laughing in the right places.

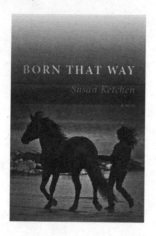 

Enjoy the funny misadventures of the dauntless Sylvia in the first two books in the *Born That Way* series.

"I love Susan's tone - there's lots of angst, but no self-pity, lots of humor...the love and respect for horses is actually rather overwhelming. We should all thank Cloudy, Lollipop and the other equines that inspired; it's a rather unique YA text."

~ Kieran Kealy, Professor Children's Literature, UBC